Unsaid

Things Left Unsaid

A NOVEL IN POEMS

Stephanie Hemphill

Hyperion Paperbacks

New York

Printed in the United States of America
This book is set in 11-point M Bell.

First Hyperion Paperbacks edition, 2007
10 9 8 7 6 5 4 3 2 1
Library of Congress Cataloging-in-Publication Data on file.
ISBN-13: 978-0-7868-3745-8
ISBN-10: 0-7868-3745-4
Visit www.hyperionteens.com

For girlfriends, old and new

ACKNOWLEDGMENTS

This book would have remained a drawer of poems were it not for the encouragement and foresight of Steven Malk, my agent and friend. I also owe an armload of thanks to Alessandra Balzer for guiding me into the story and pushing me to write my best. I am grateful to Lisa Siegel and Carol O'Day, two amazing writers, who inspire and support me from my early drafts to my finished books. Thanks to Mom for playing equal parts English teacher and cheerleader, and to Dad for being my #1 fan. But most of all I am grateful to Jim, who read this book more times than I did and conjured enthusiasm for my words on the days I needed it most this book exists because of his kindness and love.

Prologue

What you don't know is that
I have a sixth toe on my left foot

and possess superpowers,
can transform a tornado

into a birthday party,
a car wreck into a yard sale.

What you don't know is that before
this lifetime I was an oracle.

People paid gold coins to hear
my premonitions, and the flame

in my temple was tended morning
to midnight. What you don't know

is that I have always told you
the truth, covered up under

a yellow rain slicker, diminished
by good deodorant, made palatable

with crimson lip gloss. What
you don't know is that I hear

when you move your lips. I can
repeat your words in instant replay,

and my internal hard drive rarely
has memory retrieval problems.

What you don't know is that
I am a piece of glass. I see you

stand behind me, and see clearly
when I stand alone. What you don't

know is that you trail me
like a ghost. I hear you creak up

the stairs, see your outline in the mist
of my shower, feel you exhale

between my shoulder blades
when I sleep. What you don't

know is that like most renewable
resources I can be translucent

one day and broken-down
the next, sharp and then dull.

I replenish myself, shed my skin
like the rattlesnake, learn to use

new limbs like the starfish,
devour insects and enemies

like the black widow. What you
don't know is that although

my eyes appear to stare blankly
forward, words boil inside my head.

What you don't know
are the things I leave unsaid.

AUGUST ☾

Windless afternoons, slow
oppressive heat before thunderstorm,
the rapidity and eternity
of the week before
the new school year begins.

I scratch mosquito bites,
soak up available rays like a squirrel
preparing for winter famine,
and try to look forward
to whatever comes next.

Kinetic

Mom insists we shop
for school supplies, demands
I read the novels on my summer
list, rents *Casablanca*
for us to watch together.

But I try to be gone from the moment
my eyelids flutter open
till I tumble into pillow.
In a car, on the phone, my hands
open to everyone but her.

Mom barters clothes cash
for my time, but I still shut
my door, knowing she'll push
the money through the crack
and into my room, anyway.

Shopping

I'm looking for something,
new attire, layer of camouflage,
a place without color
where I fade
into surrounding scenery,
blur into darkness.

I'm tired of being the Sarah
my mother constructs,
predictable as lettuce on a diet,
ribbons in my hair, floral
nightgown, straight A's.

I want to tuck away
last year's picture of Sarah Lewis,
shop for something new.

SEPTEMBER ᕫ

stretches like one long evening,
a bronze dusk
before the weather turns gray.

The slow drag of afternoon
inside
stuffy classrooms.

I squirm in new sneakers,
feel trapped,
my desk bolted to the floor.

SAT Prep Class

Eight A.M. Saturday morning
I lug myself to the computer lab.

School is creepy on the weekend,
like a hibernating grizzly bear
you don't want to wake.
It feels unnatural to spend
Saturday morning staring
at a school computer
in a windowless room,
like I'm being punished
for ditching or causing a fight
in the cafeteria.

Gary Levy, our resident class genius,
sits next to me. He clicks quickly
through his practice test,
while I stare at question
number five so long the screen
saver appears.

Gary scores a perfect 2400—
of course he's been taking the SATs
since fourth grade, and this is my first
prep course. I tell him, "Great job."
He's quick to inform me that these
practice tests are like training wheels,
much easier than the real thing.
When he sees my sorry 1350 score
I mutter some stupid thing
about seeing what would happen
if I answered A to all the questions.
He smiles, then mentally does the algebra,
and uncovers my lie.

Amanda

Amanda grabs my arm,
"Sarah, you've got to see this!"
A group of kids has gathered
on the lawn outside the cafeteria.
Everyone points up, shields the sun
with their hands. Ten hot-air balloons
creep past the school, fueled by tongues
of bright orange flame. One basket brushes
the roof of the apartment complex
across the street. Amanda smiles at me
with a little too much excitement,
"Have you ever seen anything like that?"

Even though we are juniors, Amanda
acts pretty much like the girl
who introduced herself to me
in fifth-grade children's choir,
"Hi, I'm Amanda. I sing alto,
and I like your shoes." I glanced down
at my purple flip-flops, realized
she wore the same pair. Amanda giggled,
became my friend on the spot.

Amanda clutches her notebook to her chest,
"Wow, I wonder where they're going?"
I suppress my inclination to say,
"Who cares?" and try to imagine
how it must feel to let thoughts drift
easily out of your mouth.
Amanda can be naïve. Things she does,
things she says repeat on her
until the hall whispers,
"Amanda is a fool. Amanda is too thin.
Amanda cries in the bathroom."
The whispers sting her like wasps,
because she carries no sly comebacks
in her pocket, no shell on her back.
While Amanda looks dizzily skyward,
she misses the guy taking her down
by the knees.

Gina

Gina catches the eye
like crystal shimmers in sunlight.
One moment a rainbow,
but in a twist of wind her colors
disappear. Comedy and tragedy
perch like twins on her shoulders.

I was Gina's favorite Barbie doll:
she dressed me in the latest fashions,
braided my hair, introduced me
to all her Kens, and we wheeled
around together in senior boys' backseats.

One night I squeezed myself
into her red club dress
and the guy she wanted
asked me to dance.
I was no longer her darling.
The switch from pet to foe
a mere turn of her head,
a beat between measures.

What she fails to remember
is that she invited me into her bedroom.
I watched her wax her legs. I read her diary.
I know she fears her father like the dark.
I stood many hours in front of her dressing table,
and slept faithfully at the foot of her bed.
I know Gina like my face in the mirror,
we wear the same size shoe.

Sarah's Little Test-Taking Problem

Mr. Lonergan sends my SAT scores
home to my parents, because like
an underperforming stock, my numbers
are plummeting, I am the only
student to receive a lower score
than the previous week.

Mom freaks in a controlled
Stepford Parent sort of way,
"Are you applying yourself,
trying your best?" Dad thinks
I need better sleep, should eat
a more fortified breakfast.

They pat my shoulder, tell me
not to worry. But when I pretend
to peruse the Classifieds, I see them
raise eyebrows of bewilderment.
They have never seen me try
and not succeed before.

Next morning, Mom offers
to get me a special tutor
so that I can surrender a night
every week on top of my Saturday
mornings to studying
for this miserable test.

One part of me, Sarah of yesteryear,
is all gung ho to have a tutor,
thinks Mom and Dad are great
for shelling out the cash
to help me correct my little
test-taking problem.

Sarah Student's also a touch
embarrassed to be defective.
Clearly, I lack the standardized test gene,
require factory refurbishment.
But Mom says, "Don't worry,
no one needs to know."

Mostly I'm exhausted from critical reading,
tired of worrying about class rank,
and think a tutor makes me
like one of those grade mongers
taking gym pass/fail so they can edge
out the other valedictorian candidates.

Why do I have to care about this stupid test?

Exhausted

Monday morning exhaustion
weighs on my shoulders
like a backpack of encyclopedias.
I tossed all night, trying to decide
whether to tutor or not to tutor.

Gina is sitting on my desk
when I finally stumble into History.
She smells like an explosion
of cherry lip gloss. "You look
terrible," she says. "What's wrong?"

When I explain that I'm just tired,
she inquires about my weekend.
Rarely is my weekend as requisitely
amazing as I wanted it to be, so I'm
forced to embellish the reality

of "Went shopping with Mom,
washed the car, saw a mediocre
movie" into something stellar.
My stomach twists, panic tightens
around my neck as I search

for the right thing to say.
I shouldn't be auditioning
for Gina's approval, she is my friend
after all, but lately every question
feels like the Grand Inquisition,

as if the wrong answer confirms
my status as a total failure.
My weekend was disaster-movie
material, Mom and Dad in Superparent
costumes problem-solving me back

on the road to "Success,"
a place I don't care to visit right now.
"My weekend was lame," the words
slip from under my tongue,
"I have that stupid SAT prep class."

Gina slides off my desk as the bell
sounds. "Oh yeah, I took that thing
last year. What a joke, but it did
help me score a few hundred points
higher on the PSATs."

Resolution for Junior Year

No longer Sophomore Sarah,
the merit student,
my hand rocketing
to answer questions,

I will lower my bar.
I don't want to wear
this straitjacket
of high expectations anymore.

I'm tired of contorting
myself to fit the pattern
of straight and narrow,
perfect little Sarah.

With unpredictable success rates
my real failures will go undetected,
won't harm me, like dropped
bombs that fail to explode.

Goody-Goody

Amanda flits around my locker
after school, spastic as a butterfly
in a windstorm. She practically
foams at the mouth.

"Look!" She pulls a necklace
from under her blouse, weighed
down by an oversized ring. "Bob
gave me his ring. Can you believe it?"

No one even buys class rings
anymore, let alone springs one
on their girlfriend. The gesture
is as antiquated as "going steady."

But Amanda and Bob
are time-warped like that.
I've seen Bob carry her books,
even pull out her lab stool.

Amanda's so happy, she sparkles.
I couldn't feel more polar
opposite, but I don't want to
extinguish her excitement.

"Wow," I say. "You guys made it
official, that's great." Amanda
tackles me in a hug. "Sarah, now
we're gonna find someone for you."

I nod, though Amanda match-
making for me is almost
as terrifying as the idea
of being set up by my mother.

Amanda clutches my hand,
"You know who would be
perfect for you." She points
her pinkie finger down the hall,

where Derek Crawford squats
to empty his backpack.
Derek and I have been in classes
together since seventh grade,

but until this summer
when I spied him coaching
peewee soccer in the field near my house,
I never thought of Derek

as more than a nice boy occupying a desk.
Derek sits two rows in front of me
in History this semester.
I have memorized

the exact angle of every golden hair
gracing the back of his neck.
How did Amanda guess?
I must have swallowed a transparency pill.

Hubris

Mrs. Henry asks if anyone knows
the definition of *hubris*,
which I think pretty basic
for Honors English,
but no one raises a hand.

Last year my arm
would have waved in air,
but now I bite lower lip,
scan the classroom for someone
else to open discussion,
give Mrs. Henry a hand.

Gina flips through a pocket
dictionary, shoots her hand
forward, and elicits a smile
from teacher,

"*Hubris* is excessive pride
or self-confidence.
A kind of arrogance."

Mrs. Henry says, "Exactly,"
resumes her introduction
to Greek drama,
and Gina tilts her head
just a little bit higher
than the rest of us.

I jot down one important
lecture note: *In cases where
Gina shares my class, restraint
in scholastic achievement
no longer applies.*

Expectations

Sometimes I feel like
I might implode,
like I'm standing in a room
where the walls and ceiling
keep inching closer and closer,
boxing me in, cutting off oxygen,
compacting me down to nothing,
all the while a ticking clock
counts down the seconds
of my impending failure.

The more I think about the SAT,
the less I can sleep lately,
and the real test is literally
months away.

My alarm clock sounds,
summoning me to another
Saturday trapped in computer
room of recirculated air.
My stomach churns,
a tidal pool of anxiety,
but I autopilot myself to school.

When Mr. Lonergan says, "Begin,"
I freeze; the words blur before me.
I'm going to be sick, dash
to bathroom, lose everything
I've eaten in the last twenty-four hours
into first stall, and swear I'll never
enter that computer lab again.

On the Roof

There is a rumor on the lips,
permeating the lunch line, that Gina
almost did the unspeakable with Jackson
on his roof under a sliver of moon.

The Man in the Moon might be able to hold
his tongue, but apparently Gina cannot,
and Jackson is quick to unzip his fly as well.
They are not even dating, but the worst part

is that Gina knows I used to have a wicked
crush on Jackson Lang and today in study hall
I saw superiority lacing her "Hello, Sarah, how
was *your* weekend?" And all I can think is

whore today, gone tomorrow.
But we are supposed to be friends.

Daddy's Little Girl

Last year Gina and I played
twin sisters in the fall drama;
candy-striped identical shifts
at Good Samaritan Hospital;
and mastered the fine art
of parallel parking together.

Gina charted our weekend itinerary
with surgical precision,
kickboxing to party-hopping
perfectly planned out.
I slept as many weekend nights
at her house as my own.

Unlike the Lewis House of Tedium,
Gina's had brothers, her house
had drama. Sometimes too much.
Nearly seven feet tall,
clad in seventies metal tees,
her father terrified me.

Wardrobe aside, he's the only person
I ever saw intimidate Gina.
He'd yell, "Gina Lynn, get your
ass down here and clean up
this kitchen." Gina would shake
and dash for a mop.

One night Gina and I, giddy
after meeting a couple
of particularly adorable boys
at the movies, bounced
into her house with a tad
more volume than usual.

Her father pounded the wall.
"Cut out that racket!"
When Gina said, "Oh Dad,
calm down," he nearly lynched her
with his eyes. Gina pleaded with him
to let her take me home.

We drove without banter,
without radio. My duffel bag
of sleepover clothes abandoned
at her house. When we turned onto my street,
I asked, "Do you want to stay over?"
But Gina didn't respond.

I tried again. "Are you okay?"
"Just get out of the car, Sarah,"
Gina said without looking at me.
When I called Gina's house
the next day her dad said
she couldn't come to the phone.

Gina told me later that she slept
in her car that night, that she was fine,
and not to ask any more about it, ever.

Destructive

Clock about to strike midnight
and I'm supposed to Cinderella
myself home from Sherry's party,
so I'm not ragged tired tomorrow.

Although I vowed to end
the madness of Practice Test
Saturdays last week, Mom
and Dad persuaded me otherwise.

I tell Amanda "Good-bye,"
march upstairs like an obedient pup
to fetch my keys and coat
only to find this girl Robin

smoothing my jean jacket
over her hips. I know Robin
only by reputation, so it feels
strange to watch her prance

around in my coat, like she's
taking something away from me,
acquiring part of my skin.
Shivers cascade down my spine.

"Um, I think, that's . . .
I mean, isn't that my coat?"
I say and then wish I could
retract each stuttered syllable.

But Robin's unfazed. "Yeah,
the denim's cool." She grabs
cigarettes and lighter and bounds
out of the room. "Come on."

Robin maneuvers serpentlike
through the party. I tag behind,
eyes on my denim, and inch
my way onto the deck.

Someone has lit Tiki torches
all over the backyard,
a mini forest fire raging
above the manicured lawn.

Robin jumps off deck railing,
lit cigarette between teeth,
still wearing my jacket.
She uproots a torch

hurls it javelin-like into air
and then for no apparent reason
smashes it to ground,
smolders out the flame.

She yells, "Come on, Sarah.
Help me bust these up."
And I didn't even think
she knew my name.

Way Past Curfew

After we pockmark the lawn
with what looks like giant cigarette burns
After Robin bums me
a smoke and restrains her laughter as I choke
on my first drag
After most people retreat
to corners of the house to make out or pass out
After Gina offers
to let me crash at her place and I decline
After I have surrendered
all possibilities of attending morning prep class
After two A.M.
Robin tells me this was more fun
than the typical Friday night hormone fest
and she's glad we hung out.

Consequences

Good thing I had fun
because Mom swears
I won't see Friday night
outside our residence
for at least a month.

Usually I would apologize,
beg forgiveness, turn on
the sprinklers and try
to reduce my sentence.

But as the sun creeps
out of darkness
and the morning fog
dissipates, I see things
with new clarity.

Mom has lost
her papoose, she's not
in control of me.
I realize as I sip my Earl Grey

that she knows
that I know that unless
she chains me to the nightstand,
once I walk out the door
I can do what I want.

Fast Friends

Monday morning the cafeteria buzzes.
"Someone ruined my dad's lawn."
Sherry Lin throws her bag
on the table next to Amanda.

"That's awful." Amanda's eyes
widen. "Are you in a lot of trouble?"
Amanda looks as distraught as
the day her kitten drowned.

"You have no idea," Sherry says.
I scan the room for the nearest
exit, knowing anything I say or do
will reveal me as the vandal I am.

Robin suddenly straddles the bench
beside me. She leans toward Sherry,
"I heard it was some sophomore
computer geeks who did that to your lawn."

"Craig and Albert? I don't . . ."
Sherry shoots out of her seat.
"Oh my god. They were completely
wasted. But do you think they would . . . ?"

Robin shrugs. "Hey, you didn't hear it
from me, but that's what people are saying."
Sherry storms toward the sophomore
table, "Thanks" echoing behind her.

Robin winks at me. I think
she must be Olympian, goddess
of the well-crafted lie. She asks,
"When do you have lunch, Sarah?"

"Fifth period," I say, oblivious
to the fact that Amanda's
among us and politely
awaits introduction.

Amanda extends her hand
to Robin. "Hi, Robin,
I'm Amanda. I think you
and I have gym together."

"Right," Robin says.
She puts her hand on my shoulder
for leverage, hops off the bench,
and tells me, "See you at lunch."

"You have lunch fifth period too?"
I blather like a redundant loser.
I have to learn how to keep
my mouth shut.

Robin yells without turning around,
"I have lunch every period."

Robin

Robin dyes her hair black.
She smokes. She is exactly
the type of friend Mom
doesn't approve of: not
in the advanced-track classes,
not afraid of four-letter words.

I muster the courage to ask Robin
how she got the scar
on the left side of her mouth.
At eight months, under a baby-sitter's care,
she bit into a live extension cord.
Her parents sued, so Robin inherits
fifty grand when she turns eighteen.
Robin says college is for directionless wimps,
plans to use the money to buy a car and travel.

I tongue a small bump on my upper lip.
Eight months old, crawling around
my father's office, I ripped apart
the extension cord connecting
his pencil sharpener to the wall,
bit the end plugged into socket.
Mom says I was nearly electrocuted.

I do not subscribe to the notion
of a random universe, but believe
things happen for a reason.
You don't find a friend
who had the same freak childhood accident,
by chance. Robin and I are bonded by scar.

A scar that leaves her slightly disfigured
after three trips to the plastic surgeon,
and a scar that is practically undetectable.
Even when I place your finger in my mouth,
my scar is hard to trace.

Going Black

This season color explodes
over clothing racks—
reds, golds, azure blue.
But I gravitate past the fanfare
toward back shelf
of neatly folded black jerseys.

"Isn't this cute?"
Amanda holds up a violet skirt.

I nod, my arms weighted down
with black and gray.

My new clothes would look
the same on black-and-white film
as they do under glare of store light.

Amanda surveys my merchandise
with raised eyebrows.
"If that stuff wasn't your size,
I'd think you were shopping
for Robin."

OCTOBER ☺

The ghoul month
where things fall down
tricked to earth by gravity,
wind, dying.

Some days chill bones,
others wear without coats.
Night comes early
black as India ink

black as witch's garb.
No need for a costume,
I dress for a funeral
each day.

The 411 Exchange

Gina tells me:

that Robin is the girl who painted
the *Alice in Wonderland* set black
last spring; the stage manager
was furious and Mr. Turner
kicked her off the crew

that Robin slashed Mrs. Potter's
tires because she failed biology

that Robin punched Troy Lasserman
so hard after he called her
"burn victim," he chipped a tooth

that Robin tap dances
on a narrow gangplank, unafraid
of plunging into dark waters

that Robin is troubled
and I should walk carefully around her.

I tell Gina:

> that Robin thought an all-black
> Wonderland with glow-in-the-dark
> foliage would be a psychedelic spin
> on an otherwise boring set
>
> that Robin was out sick
> the fateful day Mrs. Potter's
> tires lost their air
>
> that Troy Lasserman deserved
> more than a damaged tooth
>
> that rumors and reputation
> are only one layer
> of the story of Robin
>
> that I was meeting
> Robin after school
> and Gina ought to come
> along and get to know her.

Snake Charmer

I feel like a lousy diplomat,
fear that I may be luring one
of my friends into a cobra's den
as I walk into Mel's 24-Hour Diner
flanked by Gina, her weapons fully engaged.

Robin lounges in a back booth
smoking Camel Lights.
Gina hates smoking.
I cross my fingers, pray
that we can all just get along.

Robin breaks out a big
Cheshire cat grin,
"So you tagged along, Gina."
Gina's shoulders stiffen
as she slides into booth, fans
away smoke hovering overhead.

I prepare for a giant storm
to erupt, hurricane of coffee
and insults hurling from one side
of the table to the other. But as I seek
protection behind my laminated menu,

Robin says to Gina, "You know
you were robbed last year,
your understudy of Alice
was galaxies better
than Norma Dodd's portrayal."

Gina smiles and says, "I know."
Gina tries to act all cool,
she flips her hair behind her right
ear, takes a sip of her coffee,
but clearly she's flattered.

Gina says, "You know,
I actually liked your black scenery.
It was lousy of them to kick you
off the play just for having the balls
to try something different."

For the next hour it's blue skies,
and shared banana cream pie.
The rain clouds calmed
by compliments. Venom unleashed
only on those not present.

Friendly vs. Friend

When I express amazement
at how well Robin and Gina
got on at Mel's, Robin shakes her head.
"I can get along with people if I want to.
I just usually don't.
But it seemed like you didn't want
Gina and me to claw each other's eyes out,
so I kept my nails to myself."

I start to apologize, explain
myself better, but Robin
covers my mouth with her hand
and tells me that most girls
in our school fall into three categories:

> Type A, Good Girls, Amanda
> serving as prime prototype,
> Type B, Barely Badasses like Gina, or
> Type C, Completely Forgettable Clones.

Robin says, "But, you and I, Sarah,
are not cookie-cutter girls."

Her lips form a wicked grin.
"Just when I've convinced people
I'm heartless, I'll guide Granny
across the street and totally
confuse the situation."

I nod my head in agreement,
though I'm not sure I'm so difficult
to typecast, but if Robin says I am,
who am I to argue?
I just better not blow my cover.

The Freedom of Robin

She stands above or below
but never dirties herself
in the toxic waste of

grades, tests, boys' attention.
Competition is for the weak-minded,
people who need gold stars

of approval to feel worthy
to breathe in air.
Robin chooses not to care,

deprograms herself
from the conformity stress
Authority Figures try to impose

on her, refuses their mold
of Robin teenager.
She tells me it's human nature

to rebel, that I possess bravery,
that the idiot drones will
Hatfield-and-McCoy themselves
into oblivion.

Straight-A Sarah

Adrenaline, heart beating triple speed,
rush of turning over essay

to reveal 98 in large red ink.
A junkie for breaking the bell curve,

the fix of a good grade
used to make me feel high

and mighty, but now I question
my addiction to A's.

Burst Balloon

Amanda corners me
in the hallway before last period.
She claps her hands like
a little toy monkey clashing cymbals,
splutters out that Derek Crawford
told Bob to ask her to invite me
to Derek's party. She finally inhales
and says, "I think Derek likes you."

I roll my eyes. Half the junior class
is invited to Derek's soiree,
someone chalked the party info
on my history blackboard.
Still the possibility that Derek
personally invited me makes me
want to turn cartwheels.
I can't wait to tell Robin, head
for the stairwell.

"Hey, wait up." Amanda races
after me. "I know you have prep
class in the morning, but . . ."

I cut her off. "No, I quit that."

Amanda looks disoriented,
like the walls are warping around her.
She grabs my arm. "Why?"

I flashback to the evening
I announced to Mom and Dad
that I would not attend prep class,
did not want a tutor
and would charcoal in SAT answers
once more in this lifetime, for practice
or for real, it was their choice.
Mom and Dad stared at me
like horns sprouted from my forehead,
their jaws unhinged.

When did Amanda start donning
my mother's white oxford,
learn to mimic her invasive tone of voice?
I shake free of Amanda's hold.
"I'm going to be late for math."

"What's with you today?" Amanda
asks, all her excitement deflated.

But I have no answer,
I just keep ascending stairs
until Amanda's nothing
but a pink blur at the bottom
of my radar.

Bad Grade

"Yes, it's a D," I say.
Mom's upper lip quivers
like she might cry or scream or both.

"What happened, Sarah?"
Mom braces herself on the fridge,
you'd think she received the D herself.

"What if I told you I just
didn't study? I don't care about
parallelograms or parabolas, don't see
why I need to memorize theorems."

I drop my load of books
on the table like a small air raid,
dart for my bedroom. Mom yells
up the stairs, "Sarah, we need to talk about this."

But I've already locked my door.
I collapse onto bed, rip my Demon D test
into perfect little squares.

I'm not anyone's straight-A robot.
I can bomb a test if I want to.
I just didn't know it would hurt this bad.

At Lunch

Amanda finishes her trig assignment,
eats five pretzels and then offers
them to the rest of us, says she's full.
When she leaves for the bathroom
Gina sticks her finger down her throat,
sneers. "I'm full." Robin laughs
and I smile, but I don't finish my apple.

Amanda returns from the stall,
chatters about the chorus concert
next week, how much she loves
the arrangement of "Shenandoah."
Robin is musically challenged,
not in chorus, and couldn't give a rat's ass.
She pulls out her nail polish, a shade of green
called Bile, and stripes her toenails.
Gina complains that Lori Alvera
should never have won the solo
because she sings like a toad, has beaver teeth.
Amanda admits Lori tends to squeak out
her high notes. Robin just says Lori Alvera
is an A-1 loser. I add, "Who'll never get laid,"

and we all laugh.
The bell rings.
We scatter down different halls,
and digest our lunch.

Mixed Chorus

Amanda warms us up on the piano.
One hundred mouths yawning open,
one hundred students pitched
on the edge of their seats,
one hundred vowels boomerang
the semicircle of the choir room.
Gina and I both sing second soprano,
but she has a private voice teacher, better
projection, and a more developed range.
Freshman year we sat next to each other,
shared music. But now I sing alongside
Caitlin Kramer. I hear Gina's voice blast
behind me, trill on the upper notes
like a soloist. In choir the idea
is to blend voices, not to stand out.
I have always been good at this,
mimicking my partner's tone and cadence,
adding my voice to the group to create
a stronger sound. I hate to sing alone,
detest my voice without the radio,
never audition for solos.
When we have individual sight-reading tests
my palms sweat, my stomach somersaults,

because my solo voice is like a pond
in early March, frozen in sections but not solid.
Just when I think I've hit a patch of smooth
steady melody, my voice cracks, splinters,
and a note slips through the ice.

History with Derek

In early morning haze
I find myself staring
as Derek stretches arms overhead,
his sweater tightening
across his perfect chest.

Derek Crawford, the peanut-butter-
and-jelly of boys, the guy everybody
likes, which is historically why
he's never entered my mind—
too bland, too sweet, too normal,
way too far out of my amateur's grasp.

When I mentioned to Amanda
that Derek looked taller, or something,
this year, she just nodded.
Why was I so mean to Amanda
when she told me about Derek's party?
The word *apologize* epiphanies
in my head, a neon sign clicked on
against darkness

at which precise moment Derek
twists around in his desk
and without provocation smiles.

I look left, scan right,
but all surrounding heads
are buried in texts, except mine.
My cheeks ignite. I quickly invest
in flipping through chapter three.

What was I thinking before
this moment? I can't recall my name.
Instant amnesia. My only thought:
Derek smiled at me.

Our Booth

Tucked away in the east corner
of Mel's 24-Hour Diner, Robin and I
slide into #28 on the seating chart.
Though SETH WAS HERE, the red vinyl booth
now belongs to us.

After school we grab a cup of coffee,
Robin's black, mine with a dash of half-and-half,
and debrief on the day's "exciting" events:
how Gina choked with laughter
at Danny Miller's heard-it-before Clinton joke;
how Amanda's gray sweater highlighted
her bony shoulders; that because my parents
refuse to grant me a two A.M. curfew
for Derek's party I will have to sleep over
at Robin's and I must absolutely wear
Robin's black leather pants to the party
because Robin is too bloated to wear them
and Derek will be captivated
by my sleek black leather figure
and have night visuals for weeks;
how high school drudges on like a life-term
and contains no male prospects
outside of Derek and possibly Jackson Lang

(though Robin thinks Jackson's
a high-order creep),
and senior year seems a marathon away.

"They should call it hell school," Robin says,
blowing a series of smoke rings
above my head. And I say, "My dear Robin,
I think you've got something there."

Hell School

A hall monitor walkie-talkies
that an unidentified student
advances without hall pass,
proper ID, or visitor's badge.
He will approach the student with caution,
all forces stay on alert. The rent-a-cops
now carry metal-detecting wands so they can
scan for weapons. We don't have to pass
a full-body X-ray to enter the building yet,
but the idea is under consideration.

Forget about ditching and getting away with it,
during kindergarten nap time
the school district installed GPS microchips
behind each student's left ear.
They can home in on anyone's location,
pull us back to class with magnetic force.

Utter the words *hate, kill,* or *die*
on school premises and you are guaranteed
a full psychiatric evaluation by the lovely
guidance staff, a phone call to both parents
"Because it is not a joking matter,"
and if a violent statement is directed

at another student or faculty member,
the administration grants you a vacation,
sometimes permanent.

But hey kids, don't despair, school officials
understand the pressures of being a teenager
today. They are here to help us through these
best years of our lives.

Derek's Party a.k.a. Make-out City

for everyone but me. I sit
on the couch like a total loser,
barely breathing in black leather pants,
and watch Gina stick her tongue down
one random guy's throat after another.
Robin drank so much in the first hour
that she vomits breakfast, lunch, and dinner
into the toilet and demands I take her home
immediately. It's not even midnight,
so the elaborate lie I wove to obtain
a late curfew backfires. I'll be in pj's
before my normal tuck-in time.
I load Robin into the car, duck back
into the party to grab my forgotten bag,
and see that Gina has moved on
from Random Guy #3. With a new coat
of red gloss on her lips, she swings
her arm around Derek's waist.

Competition

I knew that Gina would flounce around
in a short denim skirt, so I dug through my closet
for an outfit that shows a lot of leg, and spent
the requisite hour drying my hair perfectly straight.

I wonder what Gina would do if I whispered
across the lunch table that I'm mesmerized
by Derek Crawford, decide to keep my crush
to myself. But when I lose my breath
as Derek waves hello, I swear Gina's radar
senses it. She gallops across the room
with a "Hey, Derek," and they laugh together
over something she says. Gina beams
back at me as I cling to my history notes,
my Diet Coke, and look down at the Formica.

When she rejoins me she says, "Isn't he cute?"
I want to bash her teeth in, but I just say,
"I don't know. Guess so," and try hard
not to reveal anything.

Say Nothing

I resist showing the whites
of my teeth,
never smile between classes,
because happiness
can be subtracted.

Like I don't get the punch line,
I sit at my desk
not laughing, not speaking,
blanking out.

Robin's Apartment

The first time Robin invited me over, her mom
wasn't home. Heavy shadows in the front room,
that stuffed-up smell like a hatbox that's been
shelved a decade, and no sound but hum of fridge,
a stillness so complete that I believed the ficus
must be plastic, unable to breathe
in that atmosphere. I stood in the hallway,
shifting weight from foot to foot,
and scanned scenery: grandfather clock, afghan
on recliner, cordials of brandy, scotch on silver tray.
Robin grabbed coat, smokes, two cans of soda
in a mad sprint, like she didn't want to inhale.

The second time I ventured into her apartment,
Robin's mom nestled on the sofa, TV
at deafening decibels, half-gone bottle
of Southern Comfort on coffee table, glass
in one hand, newspaper in other.
I was about to say hello when Robin shushed me,
and we sneaked past her mom undetected.
Robin chain-smoked half a pack of Camels,
shimmied into jeans, removed her screen, and

taught me to crawl out her bedroom window.
"Won't your mom wonder where you are?"
I asked. Robin gave me her you're-so-foolish look,
her eyes instructing me, "Don't question this, Sarah."

Today when we turn the knob into Robin's
apartment her mom shuffles quickly past us.
The door to the master bedroom clicks locked
and it sounds like someone or something
collapses onto the bed.

Robin kicks off boots, floors it wordlessly
into her bedroom. I hang my coat, push open
the door to Robin's room. She throws
every piece of clothing from closet to floor.

"I hate my mother." Robin points to a note
lying on her bed that reads,
Your father called, 3 P.M. Call him back.

"She thinks if she never says his name,
he won't exist, his new wife won't exist,
their son." Robin crumples the paper
tightly in her palm. "Mom drowns herself
in bourbon, and then everything is fine."

With fast turn of thumb, Robin unlocks
her mom's bedroom door, hurls the note
with a "Thanks for the message, Mom,"
slams the door so hard the wall vibrates.
A mirror crashes to the floor.

Deathly and Silent

Halloween ranks
as my number-one holiday,
night of candy and trickery
and dressing up as someone else,
but this year I can't decide what to be.

Amanda and Boyfriend Bob bounce
into Jackson's annual Halloween bash
as Frankie and Annette, sculptured hair,
stiff polka-dot skirt, giddy plastic smiles.
Robin laughs and says that they
barely needed to costume to come
as a prehistoric teen couple.

Gina dolls it up as Scarlett O'Hara,
speaks with a Southern accent, fans
herself as she flirts around the room.
Robin says Gina's corseted up so tight
her backside's bigger than Atlanta.

Jackson plays gangster: pinstriped suit,
fedora, bottle of bootleg under arm,
fake .38 tucked in belt.
Robin calls his costume criminal.
"Jackson, a tough guy," she says.
"The only dangerous weapon he carries
is Daddy's American Express."

Derek drifts into the party late.
A Stetson on his head, spurs—
but his cowboy look is a misfire,
he walks awkwardly in boots.
Robin opens her mouth to unleash
some nasty comment about Crawford,
but before she spits out her words
Gina swishes to Derek's side, and we hear
her say, heavy on the Southern drawl,
"So nice to finally have a real man
at this party." Robin makes a loud
retching noise, lights a cigarette.

Robin dressed as a corpse, powdered-on
pale blue skin. Black circles ring her eyes,
a toe tag dangles from her left foot.
She convinced me to be a vampire,
sharpened teeth, blood dripping from my lips,
black pointy collared cape. A midnight
outcast, I slouch in the corner with Robin
as she criticizes everyone's attire
and our thick cigarette smoke
strangles anyone who passes by.

November

burns, an itchy throat tightening
restricting breath, speech.

Pile of ashes on the lawn
where leaves once lay.

The ground hardens, shrinks
as temperature drops

and we're confined indoors,
no lunch outside, no field sports.

Drama Club President

In charge, in control, the head of,
the leader of, the elected official of
a group of misfits; who wants the paperwork,
the faculty interaction? Gavel in hand,
Gina nods for the secretary to read
the minutes. Robin says being president
makes Gina feel important, that it's not
just an accolade for college applications
like Gina claims. I slouch in the back
of the room and don't volunteer to organize
the car wash, bake sale, or magazine drive.
I am the perennial member of everything,
the leader of nothing, not even myself.

Sometimes I wish I would stand up and say,
"Listen to me. I have something to offer
that comes from my mouth, my brain."
But I don't even choose the clothes I wear
to school anymore. The committee of Robin
casts her ballot, and the elected miniskirt
slides onto my hips. I am *always* given
advice and I am *always* taking it.

Smoke Break

Even though I don't really smoke
Robin nudges me outside,
two fingers pressed against her lips
in the cigarette sign.

My breath visible exhaust,
white as her smoking butt,
I stare into parking lot, lean back
against the Little Theater doors.

I have nothing to say,
wonder why Robin picked me,
Miss Nonverbal, droopy brown
hair stuck to my lips, for a friend.

Robin crouches on the steps,
fixates on cars idling across the street,
waiting for a change of light.
She tilts her head slightly to the left

seems to analyze the evening air,
to see something in the night sky
that is invisible to me.

Hit and Run

Amanda and Gina lean against
Robin's locker. Gina lowers her head.
Amanda balls a tissue, her eyes puffy
red. Amanda thrusts *The Sun* at me,
its headline screams FOUR LOCAL
TEENS HIT BY DRUNK DRIVER.

"God, that's awful," I say, but Amanda
searches my face for further recognition
like an FBI fingerprint program, scanning
for possible match. "Katie Suarez"—
Amanda points at her picture—
"was in children's choir. Remember her?"

"I didn't know her. I think she was before
my time." I bend to hug Amanda
when Robin pushes through us,
knocks the paper to the ground, and says,
"Can I maybe get into my own locker?"

Amanda hit squarely with stun gun, Gina
replaces her face of concern with grin
of wicked amusement. Robin shoves books
into locker, wriggles off coat, readjusts her bag.

"Don't you care that four people are dead?"
Amanda demands in her most angry voice,
which is barely distinguishable
from her frightened one.

Robin locks eyes with Amanda,
intense enough to melt her
into a puddle of butter. "So what?"

Amanda shivers. "That's so cold, Robin."

"Yeah, well, that's life." Robin yanks me
by the sleeve, motors us quickly away.

Perfect Sidekick

Like Letterman's Paul Shaffer
I drumroll on Robin's cue.

Like Peppermint Patty's Marcy
I "Yes, sir!" Robin proper respect.

Like a First Lady
I put on lipstick, but keep lips sealed.

I learn to play second man,
to roll my eyes, to scowl,

to nod or disparage on command,
to disappear from spotlight,

wipe away my shine.
I learn to hide safely behind her—

the lunar effect, light reflected,
no more pressure of being the source.

Absent Again

For the fifth time in two weeks,
Robin is missing from the lunch table,
not here to witness Gina's painted-on
jeans, not available to analyze Derek's
"What did you do last weekend, Sarah?"
Whether my name falling at the end
of his question holds secret meaning.

Robin's English teacher, Ms. Latham,
asks me if I know what's going on with her.
I shrug and say Robin just caught a bad case
of the flu. But I know Robin forges
her mother's consent over the phone
better than she does on paper.

If only my mom worked, Robin could copycat
her voice and we could both stay home,
watch movies or go shopping, and miss exams.
Miss the parade of grade mongers accosting me,
demanding my class rank, where
I'm applying to college next year.

I want to trapeze through the cafeteria
brandishing a sign that warns BACK OFF,
SLOW DOWN. We're all programmed
to move beyond light speed, shifted
into highest gear. Our buttons pushed
to fast forward.

I walk a fraying tightrope, desperate
like everyone else to cross to the other side.
The coach with stopwatch urges me
to hurry, not look back, never look down.
Robin doesn't care about reaching
the platform. She beckons jump
to the safety net, forget the rope.

Triplication

When I hang out in Amanda's bedroom,
we drink iced tea, flip through photos
of last year's musical, sing along
with Edith Piaf, swap lab notes,
and she shows me the size zero
spaghetti-strap she's wearing to Winter Formal.

When I vintage shop with Gina, she asks me
what I did with Amanda, fixates on Amanda
Size Zero, wonders if she offered any bulimic
tips. Gina discovers the most delicious sequined
bag and when my eyes tint with desire, she lets
me pay ten dollars and bring it home. In the car
she asks who I'm taking to Winter Turnabout,
says she may invite Derek Crawford.

When I cook pasta at Robin's, she devours
with ravenous appetite each behind-the-back
piece of gossip I feed her, never satiated.
Robin tells me Amanda isn't tough enough
for Drama, what do I even have in common
with her anymore? She says Gina
flaunts what Gina doesn't possess,
a rhinestone masquerading as diamond,
a waste of our time.

When I crawl into bed each night I'm left
with an aftertaste I can't mouthwash away.
In nightmares, triplicate Sarahs haunt me,
speaking three versions of every story,
and when I wake I'm never sure
I was dreaming at all.

The Park at 1 A.M.

At the playground of my elementary school
on my seventeenth birthday I swing like I did
at age six, tireless on the black plastic seat,
my hands light and loose on the metal chains,
my pigtail bumping against the back of my neck.
While my friends dangle from monkey bars
and mount the stairs to the slide, I am content
to rock through the motions of back and forth,
up and down, earth and air. I am a pumper
and a flyer astride a safe trapeze, a lone bird,
closing my eyes and lifting off. In dreams
I can fly without the swing. A few steps
in my sneakers and I walk on air, not in a float
but in flight, my arms outstretched, my body
cutting the clouds, I slide through the sky
on an invisible people mover, graceful
as a high-wire ballerina or a glider plane
or a sailboat skimming the surface of the lake.

Green-Eyed

Gina asks me if I want
to come over and help her
fold programs for the winter play,
says she'll treat me to Thai.

When I tell her sorry, I can't,
she doesn't look merely disappointed,
she looks mad, like I stuck out my foot
to intentionally trip her, and demands, "Why not?"

When I tell her that Robin and I
have plans to see this girl band,
The Blind Kittens, in the city, Gina
huffs, "Your mom is letting you go
to a concert downtown on a school night?"

When I shake my head and explain
that Mom thinks I'm studying at Robin's,
not trekking downtown, Gina loses it,
"You never used to lie to do stuff
with me on weeknights.

You're really changing, Sarah.
And catch a clue, the wannabe-bad-girl
all-clad-in-black thing doesn't fit you."
Gina slams her locker,

"I'm sure Amanda will help me."
She stomps away from me
with such force I feel a tremor
each time her heels slap the floor.

Graveyard Games

With no real Friday night plans
but half a pint of scotch stolen
from Mommy's stash, Robin orders
me to call Amanda and Gina to see
if they have anything brewing.

Amanda and Gina are just watching
a movie with Bob and Jackson, no
adventures on the horizon, but Robin
refuses to waste her buzz, and somehow
cons everyone into sneaking into the old
abandoned cemetery on Miller's Road.

We scale the twelve-foot barbed-wire
fence. Cast in midnight-blue, with large
overarching trees, the cemetery is smaller
than I imagined, a haphazard scattering
of headstones thrown onto the ground
like a game of fifty-two pickup.

We walk slowly over melting snow,
brush fingertips on marble gravestones,
squint to decipher names and ages,

try to locate the oldest grave. Brutal
winds lash our backs, my teeth chatter.
Jackson asks for a swig from Robin's flask.

Robin downs the remaining scotch
in front of him, says sorry, but it's all gone.
Bob tells the tale of the hook, Amanda
screams, and Robin cackles uncontrollably.
Gina swears she hears footsteps, and we all run,
fearing the groundskeeper might appear.

Robin refuses to run like Pamplona
with the rest of the scaredy-cats; she
holds me back and declares, "Losers,
every one of them. You could be Queen
of the Losers, except you have me."

Robin lights a cigarette, performs
an eerily dead-on impression of Bob's
stuttered storytelling, Amanda's scream,
Gina's "I think I heard something,"
and Jackson's pathetic plea for her booze.

Suppression

Lately when I'm with Robin
I print out words in my head,
examine them for flaws, rearrange
them to achieve the highest possible
score, before I let a syllable
out of my mouth. Most of the time
I abandon my words altogether,
fearing what I say will be stupid
or wrong or both.

Amanda can't blink during lunch
without Robin launching
into a criticism jag which results
in reducing bright-eyed Amanda to tears.
Now when Robin makes her infrequent
school appearances, Amanda skips lunch
and studies with Bob in the library.

Gina just dishes it back when Robin
points out a covered-up zit.
Gina and Robin bounce comebacks
across the table, compliment each other
on well-served jabs. A spectator
at their tennis match of slander,

I don't want to play—pretend
that I have a sore throat, swallow
my cough drops, and keep my thoughts
and words to myself.

Why I Like Theater

Freedom to fall into someone else,
not worry what to say

because the lines are written down,
can be memorized exactly.

On stage, I feel safe from judgment,
can step out of Sarah

drape myself in cloak of character,
play the children's game Pretend,

escape into scenario
and not look foolish at all.

Day of Internal Hellfire

Wednesday before Thanksgiving break,
day of abbreviated class schedule,
day of extended first-hour History,
day of review sheets and chatting,
day that Gina sits on my desk
constructing a list of all the guys
she kissed this year.

"Only nine," she complains.
"That averages to three a month,
what's the point of being single
if my kissing average is so low?"
I roll my eyes; only Gina would
seek a position as designated kisser.
But at least she's able to try out
for the team; my average is a big
doughnut hole. I haven't exactly needed
to reapply lipstick this year.

Gina scoots off my desk, hooks
her arm in mine, and promenades us
to Derek Crawford's desk.
Gina leans toward Derek. "So,
do you have big Thanksgiving plans?"

Derek shakes his head. "No,
just the normal family stuff."
He looks at me and smiles.
Any functioning human
would make a witty comment
about family or turkey or anything,
but I just stare down at my mules.

Gina hops onto Derek's desk,
flicks her long auburn hair
off her shoulder. "So, Crawford,
do you have plans on December fifth?"

"I don't think so," Derek says,
all his attention directed at me.
I feel queasy, break eye contact.

Gina slowly straightens Derek's
shirt collar. "Good, because you're
coming to Winter Turnabout with me."

Derek takes a deep breath. "I guess
I could do that." He looks at me,
"Sarah, are you going to the dance?"

I open my lips, but my voice
has run away. I stand immobile,
lifeless as petrified forest
and shrug shoulders. Gina just asked
Derek to the dance and he just accepted—
day I enter the ninth circle of hell.
I search for the inferno's trapdoor,
must escape back to my desk.

Gina's mission accomplished
she guides me away from Derek,
whispers in my ear, "I think
I've secured kiss number ten."

Thanksgiving at the Lewis House

is a relative mess.
My recently divorced uncle
sulks over creamed corn.
Mom swears because
her award-winning potatoes
have lumps. Dad shoves
gizzards under my nose,
and Grandpa's cup of teeth
frowns beside the crescent rolls.

Mom asks me to say grace.
I try to shake her off,
but the request is rhetorical
After mumbling brief thanks,
passing yams to Grandma,
and rolling cranberries
around my plate, I ask
to be excused.

Mom points her carving knife,
tries to guilt me into consuming
more food. "You barely touched
your turkey."

"But I'm supposed to meet Robin
in fifteen minutes." I lay my napkin
on the table.

Mom shakes her head. "Oh no.
Your grandparents would like
to spend a little time with you."

Grandpa and Grandma already
snore in the stuffing.
They couldn't care less
if I'm sitting on the sofa
as long as the TV's tuned
to *Murder, She Wrote.*

I dump my plate in the sink
and prepare for battle
when Dad says,
"Oh, let her go have some fun."

I kiss my father's cheek,
grab a coat and wave good-bye
to the turkey carcass, good-bye
to Mom.

Pumpkin Pie at Mel's

"You're late." Robin taps
her watch. I shrug and tell her
it was my mom.

Gina and Amanda peruse
Mel's menu like they've
never eaten here.

Robin slaps a twenty
on the table. "Pumpkin
pie all around, on me."

"Cool." Gina closes her menu,
slurps some coffee. Amanda says,
"That's not necessary."

But Robin cuts her off. "Yes it is.
Mom said Merry Thanksgiving,
or whatever, handed me a twenty,

and told me to take myself
to dinner. So we're having
pie and Reddi-wip."

I think whipped cream is vile,
remain the only one
with an unsullied slice.

Robin shakes the can,
smothers my pie with white
fluff, and pushes my nose

into the plate. I Reddi-wip
a white mustache on her face.
Amanda flicks a finger of cream

into Gina's hair, and Gina grabs
her by the neck, plugs her nose
and force-feeds Amanda

half a pound of whipped cream
until Amanda gags, nearly vomits.
I'm nauseated, want to ask Amanda

if she's okay, but my tongue
freezes, all my words locked away.
Our waitress Betty is less

than amused. She brings teary-eyed
Amanda a stack of napkins,
confiscates the canister,

asks us to pay our check
and leave.

DECEMBER ✎

Month of Salvation Army Santas
ringing bells, begging change.

Racing icicle lights garland
rooftops, and Bing Crosby
croons over every P. A. system.

No matter how many layers—
black turtleneck, sweater, scarf
some do-gooder tries
to warm the frozen heart.

But step outside, the landscape
shapes an inescapable gloom.
The cruel wind lashes cheeks.
Plunging temperatures frostbite
toes, and nature retreats.

Winter Turnabout

Robin and I decide to go stag to the dance,
not that we had any other option, but we act
like our dateless status is elective.

In a black strapless nightmare
that I mistakenly think I can wear without bra,
I stumble into the crepe-papered gym
just as the cover band feels the need to play
"I Still Haven't Found What I'm Looking For."
All the couples entwine. Two circles of stag
girls sway to the barely recognizable
rendition, their arms around each other
like one big group hug. I want to puke.

Amanda waves a corsaged arm,
stops dancing with Boyfriend Bob,
tells me I look great, the band's pathetic,
and she's so glad I'm here.

Robin joins us, readjusts her garter
mid-dance floor, listens to ten seconds
of the band and declares "Smoke break,
and we're outta here."

Gina pushes through a gym door,
finds Robin and me roosting on someone's hood.
"I wondered where the two Elviras
were. Didn't see you inside."
Robin flicks her cigarette. "That's
because we were avoiding you, Gina."
Gina throws her head back in a laugh,
but I know Robin isn't kidding.

Gina bounces over to me.
"Sarah, did you see how great
Derek looks in his suit?"

I stare past her at the gym door
springing open, then retreating to a close.
"We're taking off." I grind my butt
at Gina's feet and follow Robin,
already ten paces ahead.

Closet of Despair

Mom dumps a load of laundry
on my bed. "Sarah, you have more
black in your wardrobe than the rest
of this family combined." I tell her
I like black and quickly close
my bedroom door.

I hang a sixth drab T-shirt
in my closet for the color-blind.
Clothes like overcast sky—
cynical brown, maladjusted gray,
muted blue, sullen sage. There is no
cotton-candy, cherry, or turquoise,
just one sad sweater after the next.
I wonder, if you are what you eat,
do you feel like what you wear?

Flight Attendants

Robin leans against her wrought-iron
headboard, painting her fingernails Vamp—
a shade that dangles somewhere
between blood and black, and says,
"We should become flight attendants."

I nod, though a single bump of turbulence
causes my brow to sweat, my hands to clam up,
and me to hyperventilate. "What an easy job,
serving coffee and little bottles of booze,
and you get to travel anywhere for free."
Behind Robin's head is a poster of the world

plastered with red metal stars, the kind
kindergarten teachers stick on attendance charts.
A red star covers each city Robin has seen.
If I had a map like that it would be barren.
But at least no stars means no airplanes,
no trips in aluminum tombs that rattle
through the sky at thirty thousand feet.

What is Robin thinking? Stewardesses wear
god-awful navy blue uniforms, maroon
neckerchiefs, silver wings pinned across
their chests. Mom would enroll me in college
tomorrow if she thought I might push
a beverage cart for a living. Suddenly, I like
the idea of working the friendly skies.
Robin blows on her nails. The blond streak

in her otherwise jet-black hair falls
from behind one ear. I flip slowly through
the pages of *Vogue*. "Where would you go?"
Robin presses her palms together, elbows
extended, and bows her head. "To India.
They worship superior gods there, believe
in reincarnation. If you die in India
you come back as a completely different
person, start over in a new body."

I look up at her. "A new body, maybe,
but you have the same old unenlightened soul."
Robin waves her hand in front of her face.
"Sarah, you don't know shit."
The front door opens and Robin's mom
hollers hello. "Jesus, Mother, I'm painting
my fucking nails." Robin rolls her eyes.
Her mom says Robin better aim that truck-stop
language elsewhere if Robin wants to keep living
in her house, and stomps into master bedroom.

Robin pushes a fingernail into the white wall,
leaves a red stain, a small cut in the plaster.
"Like she's gonna do anything about it.
Like she ever does anything."

Snowfall

First day of winter break
and last night's blizzard
dumped a foot of snow
on the driveway.

Dad issues an edict
that I will clear the drive
solo or my allowance
will be revoked.

I shiver at seventy degrees,
detest manual labor,
and don't want to ruin
my new black leather boots,

so I trot outside in Mom's
brown ski jacket and hiking boots,
a reject from planet ugly,
and hope no one sees me.

Out of shape and sleep deprived;
each lift of shovel feels like
I'm tussling man against nature
and nature is winning.

I'm cold, sweaty, and ready
to quit when Dad emerges
stocking cap on head,
shovel in hand, to assist me.

When I was little
Dad always tunneled through
his perfect snow banks to dig
me a fort. I huddled inside

my igloo for what seemed
like hours, never cold, molding
snow chairs, sculpting snow
friends to share hot cocoa.

Now Dad and I create
small mountains around
the mailbox. Our synchronous
shovels scraping the cement.

Mom yells that Robin
is on the phone, and Dad
waves me inside, to warm up.
He'll finish the job alone.

The Ice Queen

Robin fidgets in the booth
hopped up on five cups of coffee.
She doesn't want to go Christmas
shopping, too commercial.

Doesn't want to go ice-skating
with Gina and Amanda,
too much physical exertion.
Doesn't want to bake gingerbread,

build snowmen, decorate the tree,
too expected, too family oriented.
So we drum fingers on Mel's
tabletop. Robin mashes her holiday

cheesecake into a mound of muck
not unlike the trampled, piss-stained
parking-lot snow, her fork poised
to penetrate my left hand when I say,

"We could send Gina a nasty,
anonymous Christmas card."
The *no* frozen on Robin's face
melts into a frosty nod of head.

She grabs a napkin, begins our opus,
Wishing you bad hair, twenty pounds,
and genital warts! Have a Crappy
Christmas and a Lonely New Year!

Dress Up

Robin phones me in desperation,
she needs mall support, someone
to help her manage the Christmas crowds.

Her father invited Robin to visit,
but insisted she buy something
that would pass his new wife Charlotte's
standard of appropriate holiday attire.

"You know, something your mom
would like," Robin says to me.
After Robin rejects the twenty
department store dresses I select
without even trying them on
and I witness the gargantuan line
circling the cash register, I suggest
that Robin borrow an old dress of mine—
the conservative dark green velvet frock
Mom bought me for last year's holiday concert.

Robin hunches her shoulders, wrinkles
up her nose. "I don't know. I look
pretty stupid." The dress hangs wrong
on her frame. Robin seems uncomfortable,
like she's crammed her feet into sneakers
two sizes too small.

"We could ask my mom's opinion?"
I offer. But Robin shakes her head.

"No, this is fine," she says. "It's exactly
like the stuff Dad's wife wears.
I'm just nervous about the visit,
don't want to screw things up again."

Robin lifts my bedroom window,
lights a cigarette, even though
it's below zero outside. My mom
would scream if she saw this,
heat escaping the open window,
a cancer stick stinking up her carpet.
But I choose not to burden Robin
with these minor details.

Robin says, "I haven't seen Dad
in two years, only know the baby
from Internet pictures. Charlotte's
afraid I'll be a bad influence."
She laughs, "A bad influence?
Brian is nine months old, what am I
going to do, teach him to steal toy cars?"

Robin coughs on an inhale,
can't seem to catch her breath.
She chokes down another drag,
her eyes spidery red.

Christmas Presents

On the outside the boxes
are red, green, silver-ribboned,
gold, and purple angels dancing
across the wrapping.

But inside everything turns
black as lumped coal.
Black gloves, black pants,
black crewneck, black skirt,
even a black bathing suit.

A pile of darkness surrounds me.
I try to smile, be grateful.
Mom throws up her hands,
"I thought for sure we got you
what you wanted."

As my fingers peel back
Grandma's gift paper, I secretly
hope to unwrap a little color,
and grandmas are notorious
for giving rainbow-bright gifts.

Grandmas are also renowned
for buying practical presents
like a leather-bound address book,
boring to the core
and black, of course.

December 26

Robin spends the day in St. Louis
with her dad, and Gina braves the malls,
scours after-Christmas sales.

Amanda drops by with a plate
of snickerdoodles for Mom and Dad
and a large red-bowed package for me.

I rip through paper to find
a framed photo of us circa fifth grade,
braces on our teeth, big smiles
for the camera, both of us
giving the world thumbs-up.

Deeper inside the tissue lies
a black pashmina scarf. I laugh
and push my present into Amanda's arms.
She tosses off wrapping to discover
the exact same scarf, only Amanda
winds pink pashmina around her neck.

New Year's Eve

When I get to Robin's
she's hunched in darkness,
TV flickering Times Square,
no makeup on her face,
unwashed hair limp
against her shoulders.
She chips polish
from her fingertips,
ratty sweats on her hips,
a bottle of her mother's
bourbon between her legs.

"I can't believe you're not ready.
We were supposed to be at Gina's
a half hour ago." I pull Robin's
new black skirt, price tag dangling
from waistband, from her closet
and draw her bath water.

Robin moves the bottle
slowly to her lips. The glass
clinks her bicuspids, brown
liquid drools down her cheek.
She doesn't budge.

"Come on, Robin. We're late."
It took two hours to coif, style,
and attire myself this evening,
and I don't want to miss
one more minute of the party.

"Robin." I raise my voice
above the ascending TV,
but Robin just increases
the volume.

"Fine, I'm going without you."
I turn off the faucet, hang her skirt,
slip into my heels and coat,
my hand on the doorknob

when Robin coughs up
a flood of vomit,
her body arched
like a cat with hairballs.

Tears stream her cheeks.
I help Robin into the bathroom,
my new frock splattered
with dinner remains,
hold her hair back
for the next several hours,
and listen to Dick Clark
drop the ball
between Robin's heaves.

JANUARY ◎

A new year, new calendar of expectations.
A new layer of ice freezes over the pond.

Cries of the child drowning underwater,
banging to break the surface and breathe air,
diminish to the point of being muted out.

A new beginning, room of a hundred doors
to unlock, but behind each one a brick wall.

Back to School

Everyone acts like the new year
promises change, improvement,
but we're a week from finals
still dragging around the old semester,
like a battered suitcase of hand-me-downs
strapped to our backs.

Gina repeats over the lunch table
that she can't believe
we missed her party,
it was the party to end parties,
everyone was there.
Amanda talks Ivory soap and rosebuds,

and Robin's head bends permanently
over her fingernails, never lifts
to make eye contact, not even
with me. If this is some sort
of a new beginning,
I'd better brush up on
the definition
of stasis.

The Wrong Question

Robin swirls her finger in her coffee.
She has failed to speak three words
since we arrived at Mel's.

I clear my throat. "So you never told
me how your trip to your Dad's went.
Did the dress meet Charlotte's requirements?"

Robin dead-eyes me. "Oh yeah,
the dress was perfect. We had a perfect
little time, perfect little meals, perfect
little white doilies on the tabletops,
perfect little family of three, just like yours."

I start to say that my family isn't
perfect, but Robin yells, "Shut up!"
She exhales. "Get over yourself, Sarah.
His wife wouldn't let me hold Brian.
I wasn't allowed to pick up my own brother."

I don't know what to say,
fear that anything I speak will be
held against me.

Robin unscrews salt cap, dumps
the entire shaker into her cup.
Her coffee soaks the paper place mat.

"It tasted like shit anyway,"
she says, grabs my keys,
and exits into the cold.

Just in Case I Forgot to Freak Out

Like she has nothing better to do,
Mom awaits my afternoon entrance,
motions for me to take a seat.
"Your father and I were talking last night.
The SATs are at the end of this month."

I slump down at the kitchen table.
I had momentarily forgotten
about that monster test, leave it to Mom
to reincarnate my panic attacks.
As she plods on about the books
she purchased to help me cram,
I scope the room for hidden cameras.

"Don't you listen to me, Mom?"

"Yes, Sarah. But I'm not sure I believe
that blowing off this entrance exam is really
what you want to do." She runs her fingers
through her hair. Mom looks at me
like someone swapped her Sarah
with a Taiwanese exchange student
who speaks in foreign tongue.
"Maybe I'm wrong."

I drag myself upstairs, avoid
eye contact with the mound of books
invading my desk and fall onto bed.
Who knows what I want.

Fractured

the way one side
of the face is
slightly different
from the other,
if you sliced me
in two, you would see
I am not a monarch
butterfly, that my blood
is red, but sometimes
aquamarine. There is a scar
sewing up my spine—
snip the stitches,
I dare you.

Ice Skating

I haven't laced up skates,
been on blades
for years,
and my ankles wobble
just walking on the plastic mats.

Gina flies onto the ice,
pirouettes
on one leg
like she's auditioning
for the Ice Capades. Both her blades

cut a clean forty-five–degree
hockey stop,
as Amanda and I skid
onto rink, clutch each other
in a desperate attempt to remain upright.

A five-year-old
speed–skates
past my left shoulder
and the wind off his scarf
is enough to knock me down.

Amanda topples too
and an ice referee,
the cold equivalent of a lifeguard
complete with striped shirt and whistle,
motions skaters around our mishap,

pulls us to our feet.
Amanda laughs
and I brush off my pants
when I catch Derek entering
the rink. The heat of my excitement

tilts me off balance,
and I perform
a second pratfall.
This time the referee
escorts me off ice, my cheeks a-flush,

my butt a-bruised.
Robin leans
against a locker
cigarette between her lips.
The referee points to a NO SMOKING sign.

Robin gives the kid
the finger
and he blows his whistle
like we're under air attack.
The manager shuffles out from behind

the ticket booth,
forces Robin
to leave without refund,
before the first sweep of Zamboni,
before she and I see the clearing of the ice.

Snow Angels

Fall backward
play the game of trust
and the bank will catch you.

Wingspan arms,
scissor legs
and imprint an angel.

Even if you're bundled in black,
your angel will be white
and soaring in the snow.

Robin's Ballad of Who Cares

Choking down remedial math,
surrounded by sophomores.
Every day clouds over,
but who cares.

The hallways hazed in bad cologne,
cafeteria fumes invade the stairwell,
asbestos infiltrates the lungs,
but who cares.

The slow second hand of study hall
inches forward while twenty heads
drool on desks, because
no one cares.

Chip off nail polish, paint anarchy
across your notebook
just to occupy the minutes,
because who cares, anyway.

Boredom suffocates, the mind spinning,
wound in a tangle of thoughts.
The quiet pillow overhead
that snuffs you out, and who cares?

The hole widens.
At first you claw to climb out,
but then curl, ball up, and burrow
into the sleep of who cares.

Icicles

There's a riddle
about a man murdered
by an icicle,
its sharp point spearing
his chest
and then melting
away.

Icicles dangle
from my front porch,
a row of crystal
swords.
I worry
that the noon sun
will thaw
one of them
and it will puncture
my shoulder blade
as I exit the house.

Dad usually
breaks off our icicles
with a steel shovel,
but he's
out of town.

So I scurry,
faster than gravity,
don't light
on the porch
long enough
to be wounded
by falling
ice.

SAT Saturday

1. Sarah

Six-thirty A.M., injecting coffee
I pull into Robin's drive,
whale on the horn, flip the station
for a better tune. Why is she always late?
I race up the walk, buzz her three times.
Her mom intercoms that Robin's
not feeling well, go to the test without her.
Blowing off SATs?
My mom would shave her own head
and pierce her nose before permitting that.
But this is Robin,
sick from school more than she's there.
It isn't fair.
I want to sleep, to forget college too,
but I drag myself to the cafeteria
flash ID, admission slip, calculator,
four sharpened #2 pencils,
and check into the test,
corralled with all the other oxen
this SAT Saturday A.M.
Midway through a third math section
Friday night's late cram session clocks
me over the head, the numbers blur,

one big stain on the test page,
and I lie down for a minute power nap,
awake to the warning bell with twenty
questions and two minutes left,
jealous of Robin in slippers and robe,
home. It's not fair.

2. Robin

Six A.M. gray
another freezing
Chicago weekend.
The room numb, air vacant.
Her mom still asleep, Robin peels off pajamas,
fills the tub with nearly scalding water
slips her red crayfish feet into the tub.
A full bottle of Percodan, a glass of cold water,
and a new razor blade balance on the tub's ledge.
She locks the bathroom door.

When Mom Tells Me

There's something I'm supposed to feel,
some phrase expected from my mouth,
my face should swim in a shower of grief,
but I just sit, hands folded on the kitchen table,
and nod when Mom tells me
Robin is in the hospital.
She tried to kill herself, but she's okay.

Mom wraps two arms around me, tight
as a straitjacket. My body hard immobile granite.
A crumpled tissue in hand, Mom says,
"Sarah, I'm always here if you want to talk."
I nod, tell her I know. But I want to press
the MUTE button on this whole situation.
I don't have one single word to say about it.

Check In, Check Up,
Check Out

Amanda knocks on my bedroom door.
"Sarah, I'm so sorry."

The clock reads 3:06 P.M., Sunday.
I haven't moved from bed today,
my hair tangled, teeth unbrushed.

Amanda sits down, slings her arm
around me. "Are you okay?"

I shrug away from her, wipe sleep
from the corners of my eyes.
"Yeah, I'm fine."

"Well, I feel terrible," she says with a sniffle.
"I wish I could have helped Robin."

I stare blankly at Amanda.
Amanda help Robin? Robin hardly
tolerated her and would never have accepted
any life preserver Amanda threw out.

I fall back into pillow, my eyelids
leaden. "Amanda, I'm pretty tired.
Can we talk about this later?"

Amanda nods. "Sure. Just promise
you'll call me if you need anything,
anything at all."

She wavers in the door frame,
unsure whether or not she should leave.

"Yeah, okay," I say, pull covers
quickly over head.

Third Period

Mr. Matthews lowers his lab glasses
ready to demonstrate the explosive reaction
between cesium and water, when a messenger
raps on the door, hands Mr. M a note
requesting my presence at Guidance.

I visited Guidance two months ago
for college and career planning.
Counselor Anderson glanced at my records,
asked where I was applying to school,
typed it into her computer, dismissed me.
She was Helpful with a capital "H."

Books in arm, clutching my blue hall pass,
I clack down the halls so deserted
I hear myself exhale.

Mrs. Anderson motions to the interrogation
chair, says she just spoke with Amanda,
and how was I doing? I plaster a smile,
give her my placate-adults spiel. She records
my affidavit, informs me that "Suicide is a cry
for help. We are all here for you, Sarah."

What is this, fifth-grade health class?
Like this lady in green polyester skirt
and pumps even knew me yesterday,
will remember my face tomorrow.

I'm not the one who slit her wrists.
Why so many questions, raised eyebrows,
caring nods? At home Mom and Dad
bombard me with concern, count fluctuations
in my smile, worry over my disappointment
in another night of reruns. They demand
twenty-four hours of cheery, or I'll be
quarantined to the therapist's couch.
No one trusts me when I say I'm fine.

Celebrity

Some attention at school
is good enough to pay for;
love of your new coat,
admiration for the highlights
in your hair, jealousy
because you snagged
the senior class babe.

But this point-and-stare
because my friend
tried to off herself
is not the celebrity I desire—
teacherly pats on my shoulder,
a steady deluge of "How are you doing?"

I'm spoken to
in hushes and whispers
like I'm porcelain,
easy to break,
sharp enough to cut,
and ready to fall apart.

Nightmare

Two A.M. I turn from sleep.
A tub brimming with blood,
Robin paints her toenails red.

Handprints smudge the mirror.
She punches the glass, a fist of shards
embedded under nail and skin.

The mirror splinters like a nerve.
With crimson lips, I kiss her bloody
feet. Follow Robin's footsteps, left,

then right, into the tub.
A glass of her blood
in my hand.

FEBRUARY ᓂ

Month of red.
Month of pink.
Month of closing eyes.

The shortest month
in the year.

Conversation hearts
lie on the teacher's desk,

the kind that say
Be Mine or *U R Cool,*

but all I pull
from the bag
are blanks.

Lunch Without Robin

I inch my way into cafeteria, squint
against bright overhead lighting,
sit so I face the gray outdoors.

Amanda slides so close to me
she occupies my lap, and Gina drops
her tray directly across the table.

Cornered, I open my math book,
scribble down equations, pretend to study,
anything to avoid eye contact and conversation.

Amanda covers my hand with hers.
"Sarah, we thought you might want
to talk about what happened to Robin."

I bite lower lip, shake my head,
continue copying formulas.

Gina slaps her hand over my text.
"Sarah, this is lunch, not study hall.
Prime talk time, happening now."

I yank my book out from under Gina's
hand, shove it in my bag. Cross arms
over chest, my eyes daring Gina to speak.

Gina says, "Fine, go ahead and sulk.
Act like you're mad at me. I can take it,
won't run to the bathroom and slit my wrists."

Amanda tries to interrupt Gina,
but Gina can't be stopped midstream
her fighter jet of words fly straight at me,

"The truth is Robin's little rumble
with razor blades was heavily foreshadowed.
We all knew she had problems."

Amanda snaps at Gina.
"How is this helping Sarah?"

"I'm just being honest," Gina says,
her eyes widening. "Which is more
than I can say for Robin's so-called
best friend."

The lunchroom doors swing wildly
behind me. I exit the scene so fast
it hardly seems plausible I was ever there.

Geography

Denial is the longest river
in the world
easiest to navigate
via the mouth,
but I don't utter a word.

I stand silent
jeans rolled above knees
my sneakers caked in silt
and wade into murky water
eyes closed, alone.

Dead Air

After school, I dial Good Samaritan's
psych ward. The attending nurse
informs me for the fourth time
this week that Robin is unavailable,
in group, can't come to the phone.

I ask if all my messages have been
delivered. Nurse Nancy says yes,
she believes Robin has received them.
I ask her to please let Robin know
that Sarah called again, that I miss her
and Robin can call me anytime.

As I hang up the receiver I feel
solo pilot alone, my radio defunct,
fog clouding up the cockpit,
ceiling at ground zero—
I don't know how to land,
can't tell which direction to turn
without Robin supplying my flight pattern,
worry I might be headed for a crash.

Friday Morning Stalemate—

I can't reach Robin, can't talk
to anyone else. Amanda and Bob
plead with me to go to the movies
tonight, but I decline. My weekend
promises heightened surveillance
from Mom and Dad, and not one
second of fun.

Gina and I pretend we don't share
the same classes, her voyage
into soothsaying a concrete impediment
to our speaking terms. I want to bury
my head under three-ring binder,
sleep through the rest of the day,
month, school year. But I can't bear
another trip to Guidance, so I remain
erect, try to appear alert, okay.

Derek Crawford walks toward me.
I hold my breath,
maybe he will rescue me
from my maelstrom
of questions and dread.

He says, "Sarah, I heard what happened
to your friend. It must be awful."
I slowly release breath,
clutch edges of desk, brace myself
for another "concerned" conversation.
Derek's eyes hold mine a few seconds,
then he shelves a thesaurus, returns to his seat.

Her End of the Line

I'm so happy to finally catch Robin
that I shout my heart into the receiver
only to be met with phone static.

After thirty seconds of no response
I speak louder, try to remedy
our bad connection. "How are you?
I've been trying so hard to reach you."

Robin releases a short, exasperated sigh.
"God, Sarah, all these phone calls
and this is what you have to say."

Over the past week and a half
I storehoused a trillion things to tell her,
but now I jam up, can only mutter,
"I'm worried about you."

Again Robin says nothing.
Her silence tightens the noose
round my neck.

I saved up all my sentences
in anticipation of this phone call,
toss them into Robin's wishing well,
and watch them drown among tarnished coins.

"You're pathetic." Robin speaks poison,
in the tone she designates
for people she hates. "Get a life."

For a brief second I imagine
there was a snafu at the psych ward,
that the girl on the line's other end
is an imposter. I ask, "What did you say?"

"Leave. Me. Alone," Robin articulates
each word. "You're good at that."
And she leaves me with a dial tone.

Hitting a Dead End

Robin's words knock
the wind out of me.
Why would she want
to disassociate from me?
What did I do? What
could I have done?

I flip these questions
over in my mind
like a stack of lead pancakes;
they crack plates where they land.

When I conjure Robin
in a white room, white jacket,
her nail polish confiscated,
her mind numbed by antidepressants,
I swallow the five letters of guilt.

I should have seen that she
gravitated toward black hole
and held back her coattails.
But I misread the signs,
cultivated a blind spot
for her distress.

Robin cuts contact, a brick wall
I drive into, smash head against windshield.
Dazed, I walk away from the accident,
have no one to call for help;
want to forget the whole mess,
park Robin in the back of my mind
and lose my car keys.

Don't Ask

When my uncle broke
his jaw in a bar fight
the doctor wired his mouth shut,
left only a small space
between his lips
to insert a feeding straw.
A notepad and pen hung
around his neck,
but mostly he just nodded,
his paper blank.

In volleyball, I concentrate
on bump, set, spike,
think of nothing but the ball,
ball over the net,
my feet shuffling right,
forearms contacting the white ball.
If I think only of the thing
in front of my face, ball
flying toward my nose,
I forget what's behind me.
The background blurs
and I'm fine

and there is only me
moving forward
as long as no one asks me
about her.

Next in Line for the
Psych Ward

Dad's car in garage at three P.M.,
Mom peeking through living room
curtains as I turn off ignition,
I don't need to be summoned
to kitchen table, I drop into position
as soon as I peel off my coat.

"Dad and I are worried about you."
Mom's voice sounds canned, far away
even though she sits beside me.
"You're not talking about Robin's
suicide attempt with anyone. We spoke
with Amanda, and she's worried too."

I slump down in chair, pick
apart my cuticles. Mom and Dad
don't know that the only way
I manage lately is by self-inducing amnesia.
Dad paces in front of table. He seems like
he'd rather undergo open-heart surgery

than be party to this discussion.
I concur. But Mom drives forward.
"Sarah, maybe you'd feel
more comfortable
talking to a professional,
someone completely objective."

My muscles tense up, silence
a security blanket I can't relinquish
to some stranger. "I don't want a therapist.
Please don't make me go."
My voice cracks, underutilized. "I promise
I'll talk about this when I'm ready."

I stare at my father, pray he will
take my side, but his eyes
memorize the linoleum pattern.
Mom puts her hand on my shoulder.
"Sarah, we just don't want you
to end up where Robin is."

"Don't worry," I say. "I would never
do something that stupid."

Things That Make Me Angry

Standardized tests, streets
with no parking, when the skirt
I just purchased goes on sale
the following week, fistfights,
litter, public displays of affection,
out-of-tune pianos, jarred animal
parts in the science lab, algebra,
gum under my shoe, the flu,
nightmares, unanswered questions,
playing scapegoat for someone else's
pain, blood, razor blades, lies,
anything that cuts.

Crying in the Bathroom

Sherry Lin squats on lunch bench
shaking a bottle of deep crimson
nail polish. She strokes color
onto her thumb, wheels around to say
hello to a friend, and knocks over
nail polish bottle. The sharp odor
stings my nostrils, slaps me in the face.
Thick, bloodred liquid covers the table.
All I can think about is Robin.
Nausea grips me. I stumble down the hall
to the bathroom, white-knuckle the sink.
Mascara spreads like two black eyes,
my cheeks drip charcoal. I splash water
on my face. Amanda pushes through the door,
tissue in hand, scrambles around her purse
for compact, concealer. I slump to the floor.
Amanda props her arm around my shoulders
and says, "It's okay, Sarah. Don't worry,
everything will be okay."

Mom's Lap

After school, Mom doesn't ask
about my day. She sees my sinking
lower lip, the redness around my nostrils.
Mom pours us each a mug of chamomile tea,
pats the sofa, and I lie down on her lap
like a small collie. She combs her fingers
rhythmically through my hair like she has done
for as long as I can remember.
When I wrestled with monsters
in my dreams, when a boy in fifth grade
called me geek, when in high fever
I teetered in and out of consciousness,
Mom calmed me on her lap. I know
that I am probably too old to be brushed
and babied by my mom, but today
I want to feel the safety of her fingertips,
want to feel like I'm five years old.

Apology

Note on History class door
reminds me we are meeting
in the library to research
upcoming class presentations.
I am as of yet topicless
and meander through Modern
American History when Gina
pokes me on the back. I pretend
not to notice, slink down the aisle,
but she's on my tail like Velcro,
whisper-screaming, "Sarah. Sarah, wait."
One finger to lips, I shush her,
sit down, leaf through *A People's
History of the United States.*
"Sarah, I feel bad. I should never
have said that stuff in the cafeteria.
What do I know about being
a good friend when someone's in trouble?"
The librarian informs Gina
that there is no talking.
Gina scribbles, *I'm a jerk, a creep.
I'm sorry. Please forgive me,*
pushes her spiral across the table.
My impulse is to crumple the note
and ram it down her sorry throat,

but Gina repeats, "I'm sorry, Sarah."
Her voice echoes across the stacks.
The librarian swishes over to Gina
so fast her reading glasses pendulum.
She demands evidence of Gina's research
this period. Gina says, "I've been looking
into the Society for the Preservation
of Important Historical Friendships,"
flips through a book. "See here,
on page twenty-three it says, apologizing
when you pick on a friend in need
is key to friendship survival. So excuse me,
but I need to get back to work."

V-Day

The most dreadful day
on the calendar,
a long syringe of sugar
forced down our throats
until we choke on granules.

Half the girls in homeroom
are pinked up,
red hearts dangle from earlobes,
chocolate dribbles down lips.

The JV Poms knock
and Mr. O'Dell ushers
them in to pass out
candy-grams and butcher our names,
Adams to Zolvsky, pronounced
with foreign phonetics.

Pom #2, hefty rhinestone heart
between her breasts, breathes
a sigh of relief and calls out,
"Sarah Lewis," and I have to trot
to the front of the class
to retrieve my candy-grams.

Pom #1 bends over just enough
to entice with her upper thigh.
She rifles through a red plastic bin
and deposits three candy-grams in my hands.

The first is from Amanda.
Sarah, you're such a great friend
with SweeTARTS attached.
Gina's salty, tapes a Tootsie Pop
to the paper, and says, *Love sucks.*
Valentines suck. Enjoy the candy.

If things were normal the third valentine
would be from Robin. I miss her.
Her absence feels palpable, like oxygen
extracted from my air supply.
Robin would offer welcome counterpoint
to today's commercial celebration
of the ludicrous and the lovebirds.

I slowly flip over third candy-gram,
the humdrum block print begins
HAPPY VALENTINE'S DAY,
but has the inspired ending
of *Derek Crawford.*

The red heart-shaped lollipop
fastened to the paper
makes my cheeks flambeau.

Am I doomed to join ranks
with the loons and the lovestruck?
I tuck the sucker in my backpack
too good to eat.

Old Habits

Like a sleepwalker
I can navigate
even when my eyes
are closed.
My feet follow common
carpet tread,
negotiate stairs with ease.

I'm half asleep,
wading through the wake
Robin created.
I sink into Familiar Sarah,
the one who studies,
the one who doesn't break
curfew, the one
I hope no one needs to worry about.

Acting

Depression, according to *Webster's*,
is "emotional dejection, sadness or gloom
greater and more prolonged than warranted
by any objective reason."

In acting class, Barb Lindo asks me to play
the lead in her one-act. If I had never
been friends with Robin, she wouldn't
dare approach me. Barb tromps around
in black steel-toed boots, spikes her short hair
like a leftover from the punk rock scene,
and has a tattoo on her right tricep that says
FUCK OFF.

When I read in her script, *Autumn,*
that the main character suffers date rape,
an abusive father, self-absorbed friends
and offs herself with bottles of vodka
and codeine, I understand why Barb *thinks*
I will be so perfect for the role.

By wearing a sullen black turtleneck,
wan complexion, and dark penciled eyes,
I convinced everyone that after Robin,
the second definition of depression
held a picture of me.

I deliver the final soliloquy
well enough to induce tears:
"It's autumn turning sharply toward winter.
Cold and barren, I turn to no one.
Have nowhere left to go, but to sleep."
But these lines were written
by someone else, about someone else.
Everyone should know they're not mine.

Deceptively Simple

Passing period, Derek crouches
at his locker loading backpack
with afternoon books. I want
to thank him for the candy-gram
he sent last week, but my cement
feet won't cooperate.

Derek and I have yet to engage
in a call-and-response conversation.
I never manage to compile more
than three words when he asks
me a question. I just nod, smile,
duck out of room, and then bang
head against locker for suffering
from momentary muteness.

I have a perfect opening,
"Thank you," should shuffle
over to Derek and say it.
Thank you? Not exactly an original
phrase. Surely I can figure out
something snazzier to say,
like *How sweet of you to send candy*
or *Loved the sucker.* I snap together

different phrases in my head
until I'm reeling. I gag on my words,
all my combinations sound wrong.

Derek closes locker door.
He notices that I'm ten feet away,
watching him. He smiles, starts
to approach me. I bite fingernails,
what should I say? The bell blasts
overhead. Startled, I quickly wave
good-bye, dash down hall to next class.

The Nuthouse

I sign my name on visitors list,
slap a HELLO MY NAME IS sticker
on sweater, hold my breath as I'm filed
through antiseptic corridors.

The visiting room stark and beige,
fills with stripped-down patients
and their whispering family members.
A girl with frizzy orange hair
catapults from subject to subject,
one minute complaining to her mom
about the subhuman food, the next
whimpering that the hospital sequestered
everything, her bathrobe, her shampoo,
her makeup, her magazines.

I look around the room scattered
with pale apparition-like girls,
wonder if the hospital locked
their real bodies in a closet
to be returned only when and if they leave
the ward. Twenty minutes of visitation
hour tick away and it dawns
on me that Robin may be a no-show,

that the tag over my breast should
read HELLO MY NAME IS NOT WANTED.

A nurse announces that the patients'
group therapy commences in five minutes,
all visitors must leave. I fixate on the door
sealing off the psych ward, hope to catch
a glimpse of Robin's deep black hair,
but I don't.

Breaking Down

Already twenty minutes late
for study group at Amanda's
I pray for no traffic, no cops
looking to reach end-of-month
quotas and nab speeders

when I hear a loud, but contained
explosion, like someone popped
a paper bag under my front tire.
The car swerves. I smell molten
rubber, sparks jump toward my

windshield. I curb the car. It must be
twenty below and I am exactly
equidistant between Amanda's
home and my own, multiple miles
to traverse in either direction.

The car sags on driver's side
like a sad three-legged dog.
Tire shriveled. I kick the skeleton
wheel with the heel of my boot.
Pound fist into hood, *Why! Why! Why!*

I should just abandon this stupid
car. Anger swirls, twists around
my head, accumulates exhale
by exhale. How could my car fail me?
I didn't even know the tire was deflated,

let alone about to self-destruct.
Tears pool on my scarf. Another kick,
and I stomp toward home, pull out
mobile phone, and call Mom. "Mom,
I'm so angry. I mean I'm really MAD.

The tire blew out. It just destroyed
itself for no reason." Mom tells me
to calm down, she's on her way.
But I'm shaking and it's not
temperature related.

Breaking Down: The Sequel

Maybe it's being alone, immobile
at the side of the road, an arctic wind
lapping at my ears,
maybe it's the reminiscent dial tone
clanging in my brain after Mom hangs up,
maybe it's the image of Robin's
empty visiting-room chair
that I can't shake,

but when Mom picks me up
my lockjaw ceases and the novel
I've held on reserve pours from my mouth.

I tell her about the phone call,
the psych-ward excursion, the nights
I can't sleep because dream after dream
I stuff pills down Robin's throat, draw
the razor across her wrist. I tell Mom
about the waking moments I tremble
knowing how close I came to falling
into the same manhole Robin tumbled down.

I crumble onto couch,
sob ten straight minutes
until my tear ducts run dry,
lean against Mom, match my breathing
pattern to hers, and close my eyes.

Spring Cleaning:
Letting Some of It Go

I have spent cold months
crouched in a dark closet,
light turned off. It's a midnight
I can't hold on to anymore.

I want to start clean.
I weed through my closet,
fill the garbage bag at my feet
with a thousand shades of black.

Black, the color
that devours all light,
speaks in shadow or echo
or says nothing at all.

I empty my hangers
of silent winter grays,
need to make space for a range of colors,
bag the old stuff for Goodwill.

MARCH ♫

There is this word
on my tongue—
verdant

which means green, lush
or in a person
unsophisticated.

Green things can bud
simply, require only
rain, seeds, sunlight.

Anesthesia wears off
and the mouth opens
to drink, speak, recover.

It's Good to Be Drama Queen

Gina bounds into cafeteria,
"Guess who knows what the spring play is?"
She leaps into seat. "Inside info, the best
part of being Drama Club president."
She unwraps her turkey sandwich,
then holds up two fingers
like she's taking the Girl Scout oath.
"Of course, Mr. Turner made me swear
not to tell anyone." Gina motions
for Amanda and me to press in close.
She megaphones her hands around mouth
and whispers, "So I'm not telling you
it's *The Miracle Worker.*"

Amanda gasps. "That's so great.
Lots of good female parts."
Gina nods and smiles. "I know."

Spring play—I forgot the year's
big stage production lies on horizon.
The possibility of a new role to play
spreads a large grin across my face.

Gina points at me. "A little gossip,
and look, she smiles."

Under This Skin

I itch,
not pathologically,
but like I'll feel great relief
if I untie my wool scarf

and let my neck bathe
in sunlight.
I'm ready to take
something off,

shed the heavy layers.

A Beginning

In choir, there is one part in the song
"Summertime" that none of the second
sopranos can seem to hit—a minor note
in a major phrase like a lone violet petal
among yellow daisies.

Mr. Jordan taps his baton, plunks
our note on the piano, and says,
"Concentrate, girls." I can hear the note
pitch-perfect, but hesitate to sing up,
don't want my voice out there on its own.

As we roll toward the tricky measure
I close my eyes. The other girls
in my section decrescendo, and I hear
my voice by itself, clear as a tuning fork,
for a moment. My music partner, Caitlin,

blends her voice with mine
and the rest of the second sopranos
follow. Mr. Jordan smiles at our section.
"Nice job, girls. Now that wasn't
so hard, was it?"

Hallway Between Guidance
and the Little Theater

I pick up a fallen poster
announcing *The Miracle Worker*
auditions and try to stick it

to the wall, but the tape gives way
and the poster slides to my feet.
Someone asks, "Need some help?"

I turn around. It's Derek Crawford.
"You have a roll of tape?" I say,
abandoning my usual hesitation.

"No, but my French class is just
down the hall. Wait a minute."
Derek returns with masking tape,

secures the poster's corners
as I hold the middle, our bodies
an inch from actual contact.

"Are you auditioning?"
he asks as he steps back
to admire his work.

"Um, yeah. I mean . . . I
think so . . ." I stammer,
look down at my sneakers.

"That's great. I could never
get up in front of people like that."
Derek leans one arm against the wall.

I shake my head. "It's nothing.
I mean we're just a bunch
of drama dorks."

"No, it's cool." Derek looks
directly into my eyes. A big
grin stretches across my face.

"Well, I better get to class.
I'll see you in History," I say,
and after Derek turns around

I practically dance down the hall.

The Practically Perfect Day

On the kitchen table sits a mocha,
my favorite from Java Café, twenty
dollars, and a Post-it that reads *We Love You.*

My hair dries in ten minutes, shiny, straight.
The scale registers two pounds less, and I'm
not dieting. All green lights guarantee

a space in the student lot. Aced my *Crime
and Punishment* paper, Mrs. Henry
pencils in *Excellent writing, Sarah.*

Gina compliments my new platforms, and
Amanda warns pop quiz in Chem. Derek
places his lunch tray, unprovoked,

on the table next to mine, raves about
my Iran-Contra report. His gray-blue
eyes follow my smallest movement, the arc

of my breath, as though we're wired together.
His hand brushes mine when he recycles
my soda can. He says he'll call me, if

that's okay. I flit down the hall.
Little flecks in the tile catch sunlight.
I walk on silver. Mr. Turner clears

his throat, reminds us this year's final
production is *The Miracle Worker*, auditions
in two weeks, and I swear he winks at me.

Gina and Me at Mel's Diner

I ask the waitress for nonsmoking,
Gina nods approval. Neither of us
wants to sit in the regular booth.

Gina orders a chicken sandwich,
another deviation from our usual
shared slice of banana cream pie.

"It's weird without Robin."
Gina swirls milk into her coffee,
softens her voice, almost whispers,

"Are you okay, Sarah? I mean
you seem okay, are you?" Normally
I want to toss hot liquid at anyone

who asks if I'm okay, but today
it doesn't bother me, maybe because
Gina sounds like freshman year,

her voice a best friend I miss,
or maybe because the answer
is yes, I'm okay.

"You're auditioning, right?"
Gina's tone mutates from concern
to hard, cold cement. "I just love

the lead, Annie Sullivan, don't you?"
So we're back in the ring, scavenging.
I grind my teeth, "It's the best part."

Gina's lips curl slightly at the ends,
"I think Derek Crawford likes you."
A toss of her mane and she leans in,

"You can have him, definitely *not*
my type." The waitress must have
dumped sweetener in my coffee.

I smile at Gina, and without a hint
of spar reply, "Good, because
I think he's pretty cool."

After-school Routine

As soon as I unlock garage door,
Mom calls from laundry room,
"Sarah, is that you?" as though people
indiscriminately wander into our house.

We powwow at kitchen table
and Mom inquires about my day:
what's the homework situation,
what after-school activities
are calendared this week, how's
Amanda, what's Gina up to, does the car
need gas, how am I doing, how am I
feeling, any news of Robin?

I tick off answers to Mom's questionnaire.
It's better than spilling my innermost
thoughts to some note-taking stranger,
but I'm not exactly in love with the hot seat.

Mom grabs something off kitchen counter,
"I picked this up at the bookstore.
Thought it might help you with auditions."
I smile, flip through *The Miracle Worker* script,
"I tried to get this from the library today,

but all the copies were checked out.
Thanks, Mom." There are advantages
to keeping Mom in the loop.

To Buy or Not to Buy

Amanda and I scour
Marshall Field's in search
of appropriate attire
for next week's spring concert.

The dress department
is crammed with fifty versions
of the little black dress, and I'm drawn
like Pavlov's dog to every one.

Amanda carries an armload
of greens, blues into fitting room
when a little red number
across the aisle catches my eye.

Not only is it A-line,
knee length, and cut to flatter,
but it's on sale. All the other dresses
draped over my arm look

like something already hanging
in my closet. I slither into black
sheath after black sheath until
I can't tell which I've tried.

Amanda yells, "Think I found it.
How about you?" I mutter,
"Uh, well . . ." and emerge from stall
in the red dress. Amanda gasps.

I twirl around, examine all sides
in three-way mirror. The dress
breathes on my frame. I can't
come up with one reason

to dislike it, except that it's
RED. Amanda threatens, "If you
don't buy that, I'm buying it for you."
I smile, head into dressing room

to change. Second thoughts
creep into my skull. Red is
the look-at-me color, color
that screams, the color of blood.

Maybe more color
than I can handle right now.
I pick up my purse,
leave the dress behind,

but then whisk it off the rack.
Maybe a little red
is exactly what I need,
and if not, I can always return it.

Please Pass the Test Results

Mom hands me the spinach salad
and says, "Your SAT scores
should have arrived weeks ago.
We think the College Board
lost your results."

I smile, it feels karmically correct
for my scores to have been misplaced.
SAT Saturday detached itself
from exam as soon as I learned
about Robin, has associated
in my mind only as the day
of her attempt. No one badgers me
about class rank or test scores anymore.

"I fell asleep in the math section.
I'm sure my score is awful,"
I say and try to restrain my laughter.

Dad says, "You think that's funny?"

I try not to giggle, take a sip of water,
but the memory of waking up
in a pool of drool with two minutes
to finish the test sets a laugh

bubbling out of me. I spit-take
a mouthful of water at Mom.
She wipes brow, then explodes
with laughter.

Dad sets down fork, perplexed,
"You two are nuts. This is serious.
They've lost Sarah's scores."

Mom says, "Maybe their loss
is a blessing in disguise."
Dad's face twists into question mark.

"I think I should just retake the test,"
I say between bites of wheat roll.

Mom smiles and Dad says,
"An excellent idea."

On the Way to the Concert

In the red dress, concealed
by black leather jacket,
I pick up Gina and Amanda.
That heinous disco song
I Will Survive comes on the radio.
When I flip the station, Gina tunes
it back in. "That's an awful song,"
I tell her, but she and Amanda

belt out Gloria Gaynor, like a couple
of rock divas. "Lighten up, Sarah,"
Gina says between verses.
Amanda transforms her cell phone
into microphone and we each sing phrases,
bounce and bop until the car quakes.

At the stoplight a young couple stares
at us like we're circus freaks. Gina jumps
out of the car and in a grand display of 1979,
shakes her moneymaker and everything else,
to the couple's consternation, my hysteria,
and Amanda's applause. They pull away.
Our voices boom against the night.

Ventriloquist

After midnight, avoiding my *Othello* paper,
tired of practicing sign language
for Friday's audition, I flip channels,
come across a ventriloquist on cable access.

The balding man props a plastic plaid-suited
mannequin on one knee. With each throw
of voice, the ventriloquist tightens his smile,
beads of sweat on his gleaming scalp.

There is something creepy about the chomp
of the mannequin's lips. His master, like a devil,
widens the doll's mouth through a hole in back,
completely controlling his language.

In *The Miracle Worker*, Annie Sullivan
teaches Helen Keller a way to stop playing
mannequin, break her cage of silence, darkness,
and share her voice, her vision with the world.

Nothing inhibits my language, yet I often
choose to be the plastic doll on bended knee,
throwing other people's words out my mouth.
Why do I surrender my voice like that?

Reclamation

Searching for one lost strappy sandal,
I come across the denim jacket
Robin admired and quarantined
the night we first hung out.

I slip into the coat,
it smells like Camel Lights,
feels battered, foreign.
I remove coat, cradle the denim
to my chest, and inhale Robin.

The jacket doesn't seem like
it belongs to me anymore.
I toss it into washer, want to
rinse out the cigarette stink,
make it smell like my perfume again.

When I pull jean jacket
from dryer, the color's faded,
not the same shade I wore last year,
but it also doesn't smell like Robin.
The frayed sleeves show use.

I stitch a ripped buttonhole,
slip into my coat. It fits me
in a different yet comfortable way,
almost like the jacket's new.

Sometimes I Think Maybe I Am a Lousy Friend

because truth be told, I'm happier today
than I have been in months.
It's as though I've been wearing
a fifty-pound sweater of gloom all winter
and now someone has pulled it off me.

When I walk down the hall and people say,
"Hi, Sarah," I smile without reservation.
For half a year SarahandRobin were
conjoined with such consistency
that I was beginning to believe
my name contained five syllables.

Today in History, Derek asked me
to go to the movies. If Robin were around
I would have asked her opinion
before answering Derek, as though my lips
worked only when she filled them with words.
But today I just say, "I'd love to."

Spotlight

Robin shielded me
from blistering heat of spotlight,
blocked me from audience view,
then abandoned me to bake
under glare of inquisition
about what happened to her.
But now that bulb flickers,
is burning out.

Bright electric globes
tossed onto stage
entice me.
I trace edges of spotlight
not sure if I'm ready
to stand in that much visibility
by choice.

Tired of my shadow
movements,
I inhale deep,
visor eyes with hand,
and inch into ball of light.

Auditions

Everyone auditioning
for Annie Sullivan or Helen Keller
has to read the final scene,
the play's emotional climax
in which Helen learns
that language exists, and speaks.

Mr. Turner randomly pairs off
Annies and Helens, gives us
fifteen minutes to rehearse
with our scene partners.
Unfortunately, there aren't enough
Helens to go round,
so Debbie Donovan is assigned
to read with me after
she performs with Lisa Frudle.

I sit on steps and watch
Lisa and Debbie block their scene.
Mr. Turner calls us in before
I have a chance to practice
one line with Debbie.
Debbie apologizes. I tell her
not to worry, that I'm an intuitive
actress. But secretly I'm terrified,

slink down in auditorium seat,
my fingers so stiff I doubt
I'll be able to sign a single letter.

Gina and her partner volunteer
to go first. Gina says that way
she's never intimidated by other
performances. Gina nails the signing,
hits all her marks, sets the acting
bar high for those who follow.
She exits the stage, smiling.
I mutilate my cuticles,
keep reversing lines in my head,
each successive audition seems
better than the last. I decide to sneak
out theater back door, save
what little remaining dignity
I possess and not try out at all,
when Mr. Turner summons me to stage.

I wobble up proscenium stairs,
feel like if I open my mouth
I'll lose my lunch.
I want this role that bad.

I step onto stage, find my starting
position, close eyes,
and momentarily forget Sarah
and all her neuroses. Mr. Turner says,
"Whenever you're ready, girls."
And Annie's eyes open into spotlight.

APRIL ⟲

breaks open
    like an egg

shakes off shell
    flaps wings

stops looking
    down

anticipates
    cloudless sky

eyes wide
    on ascent

The Cast List

Eighth period, three minutes
until end of day, the second hand
appears stalled. Two flights of stairs
to the theater doors. I squirm in my seat.
Lisa Frudle packs her bag, half her body
already down the hall, so at least I'm not
the only anxious one. The bell!

I slow my pace, an actress acts
calm, not overly eager. Still
my heart jumps against my sweater.

A crowd circles the bulletin board,
the list posted. One girl in tears
retreats down the hallway, her friend
assuring, "There's always next year."
I sidle up to the group, two guys clear
a path, but all I can read around Jay
Sherman's six feet is *The Miracle Worker*.

Amanda weaves through the crowd,
"Have you seen the list?" I shake my head.
She tells me to go see it for myself.

I'm ready to knock people out of my way
with heavy blows from my backpack,
when I reach the white sheet.

In Times New Roman, top billing,
ANNIE SULLIVAN . . . . SARAH LEWIS.
I try to suppress a smile, but can't.
Amanda throws her arms around me.

Two Phone Calls

I pull car door closed,
can't stop bouncing in driver's seat,
don't mind that the student lot's
gridlocked, that cars jam me
into my spot. I speed-dial
the one person I know will be
as happy as I am about the play,

"Mom, you won't believe this,
but I got it. I'm Annie Sullivan."
Mom releases a yelp, then stammers,
"Sarah, that's . . . Wow! That's great.
I'm so happy for you."

Mom lets me blather five uninterrupted
minutes about *The Miracle Worker*.
She suggests we surprise Dad,
pick him up from work, celebrate
together at the restaurant of my choice.

I pause, "Actually, Mom, could we
do that tomorrow? I kind of wanted
to see if . . ." Mom says, "Sure, we'll
celebrate later. Go be with your friends."

I thank her, hang up, click through
address book, and dial a new number.

"Hi, it's Sarah," I say.
"What are you doing? I mean,
can I come over and see you?
I have good news."

Derek

lifts me off his front porch when I tell him
I'm playing Annie Sullivan, as if his name
were the one printed on cast list. Derek
plays soccer, has never set foot on stage,
but he asks if I'll teach him how to sign.

Derek spreads a blanket in the field
behind his house. Clouds like cotton balls
cushion the aqua sky. We share a deli sandwich,
lean back on elbows. Our shadows lengthen
with the afternoon. Derek so close to me,
I smell the clean scent of his T-shirt. Wind
rustles the white birches, Derek's hand strokes
my arm, my neck, my cheek, one finger traces
my lips. His lips soft, tender. He takes my hand,
spells slowly into my palm, BE MY GIRLFRIEND.

The Replacement Dance

I am
switching partners,
not destined to disco
with Gina or stage dive Robin's
mosh pit,

Derek
asks me to slow
dance. But in wrapping arms
round his waist, I waltz away from
my friends.

At My Locker

Amanda posts a banner,
CONGRATULATIONS SARAH,
the first letter of my name replaced
by a hand-drawn fist, the sign for "S."
Amanda volunteered to be stage manager
for *The Miracle Worker*, wants to learn
how things operate outside the spotlight.

Down the hall, a sign covers Gina's locker.
She plays Mrs. Keller, a substantial part,
but not what Gina wanted.
At the read-through Gina hugged
and congratulated me, offered
to run lines together, but as she spoke
she stared at the theater's exit sign,
avoided direct eye contact.

I shove my chemistry book into my locker,
turn toward Gina, want to halt the expanding
chasm between us. Derek's arm wraps
around my waist, I yelp with surprise.
"Come on, I want to show you something,"
Derek tugs in the opposite direction of Gina.

Gina glances briefly our way, shuts
her locker door, and dashes off
before I can wave hello.

Annie Sullivan Was Haunted Too

Lying on my bed,
highlighting my lines, wonder
how I missed the part

about her brother,
Jimmie, the one who dies, his
voice forever lodged

inside Annie's head.
How did I read through the script
and not see her loss?

Double Date

Late Friday afternoon
my hand aches from writing down
Mr. Turner's elaborate blocking
of Annie's arrival at the Keller house.
At one point the script dictates
that Helen whack Annie so hard,
Annie spits out a tooth. Mr. Turner says
we'll plant a blood capsule on set
which I'll break open inside my mouth
when I spit out my fake tooth.
Just the mention of blood
and my knees wobble. I grab desk chair,
want to protest. I hate the idea of fake blood,
of tricking the audience into believing
I'm in pain. But as I brace myself on chair,
regain equilibrium, I remember we're producing
a stage play. This is Annie's blood, not mine.
I have no claim to it, no responsibility.

After rehearsal, Amanda looks as dazed
as I am, her stage manager's notebook
crammed with a million lighting cues,
a ten-page list of necessary props.

She shoves papers into her bag,
"What are you doing tonight?" she asks.

"I'm supposed to call Derek,
and then I don't know," I say.

"You guys should come bowling
with Bob and me. I never see you
outside of rehearsals." Amanda peps up,
excited by the prospect of a double date.

I nod, tell Amanda okay as long as it's fine
with Derek, catch Gina in peripheral view,
gathering her coat and bag. She must have
overheard our whole exchange.
I should walk over and invite her along,
but she and I are still on the outs, stepping
around each other like you avoid broken glass
on the sidewalk. I'm tired,
not sure I possess the requisite energy
to mend a ragged friendship tonight.
The excuses mount in my head
like dirty dishes piling the sink, and
when I finally turn to Gina, she's gone.

New Seating Chart

Derek sits next to Amanda.
As I approach the lunch table,
she says to him, "I had no idea
you were such a bowling pro."

Derek shrugs. "My dad used to
drag us to the alley every Wednesday
night when we were little. Guess
bowling's like riding a bike,
once you acquire the skill you're set."

Derek smiles, asks if I want him
to grab me a soda from the machine.
I nod an emphatic *Yes*. As soon as
he leaves the table I inquire as to
Gina's whereabouts.

Amanda says, "Gina claimed she had
Drama Club errands to run, but I think
she feels awkward around you and Derek."
I release the sigh I've been holding
all morning. "What do I do, Amanda?"

Amanda shakes her head. "I honestly
don't know." I stare over at Derek.
I should possess the answer to the Gina
puzzle, she's one of my best friends.
I scratch my head, wish I could read minds,

know the right thing to say to her.
Derek returns to table armed
with Diet Coke and a funny story
about plumbing trauma in the boy's
locker room. I sip my soda,

decide to reel in my anchor of worries
and sail along with Derek's
good mood for the rest of lunch.

Derek Doesn't

lavish me with gifts, no bouquet
of flowers tucked under arm,
no extravagant city dinners,
elaborate weekend excursions,

but when he phones, e-mails
after midnight, Derek asks
how I broke my arm when I was five,
my favorite literary character,

best song lyric, most ticklish spot,
which city I find alluring.
The next day he slips a postcard
of Florence through my locker slats,
Someday Soon inked on back.

Act II: Running Away

To rehearse the scene
where Helen refuses to eat
properly at the dining table,
I strap knee and elbow pads
over old sweats, suit up
like a contestant on one of those
"test your fear" reality shows,
like I'm prepared to bungee jump
off the side of a skyscraper.

In the scene, Annie physically
forces Helen to sit in her chair,
use a spoon, and fold her napkin.
A battle between stubborn girls,
food flies across set, but Annie
remains steadfast, determined to teach
Helen Keller some manners.

I tackle the freshman girl
cast as Helen, pin her back
into her seat for the fifth time.
My arms cross over her chest,
confine her to the chair.
She bites my hand, breaks free
of my constraint. I run after her,

but instead of running after Helen
suddenly I'm chasing Robin,
holding Robin down, dragging
Robin back into place.

I lose concentration. My arms
fall limp and Helen springs
from chair, scampers to the set's
locked dining room door,
the one place I'm supposed to
keep her from reaching. Mr. Turner
tells us to stop, take a break.
I must be tired of restraining Helen.

I lean against brick stage wall,
curl my knees into chest,
catch my breath.
Could I have held Robin tightly
enough to have stopped her?
And what would have happened
if I had?

Gina stares at me from the auditorium's
back row, when she catches me
looking at her, she buries her nose
deep in homework. I must have contracted
leprosy in the last month, Gina dodges
me like I'm contagious.

Mr. Turner calls positions,
and I trot back to dining table,
tighten kneepads, and prepare
to handle Helen.

Identity

Falling again
into pattern of someone else,
a twenty-year-old, half-blind,
nineteenth-century schoolteacher,
a costume well suited to wear
on stage, but nowhere else.

Annie Sullivan's words cram
my mouth, roll easily off my tongue.
I have many of her lines
and movements memorized now,
and it feels comfortable
like lounging in oversized pajamas.

Sometimes it feels easier to play
Annie than walk through school halls
in my own sneakers, and it kind of
freaks me out. Sarah isn't a role
I've been cast to play, specific
lines and actions I can memorize.

I'm not some simple combination
of Mr. Turner's lead actress,
Derek's new girlfriend, Gina's
Barbie doll, Amanda's framed photo,
Mom and Dad's successful daughter,
Robin's lost sidekick.

Toss those ingredient parts
into blender, push mix,
and you don't end up
with the recipe for Sarah.
I total more than those things,
parts not greater than the whole.

Where's My Miracle Worker?

Rehearsal exhausts me, the physical
tantrums between Annie and Helen
amount to more aerobic exercise
than I have engaged in in my entire
high school career.

Gina barely says an unscripted word
to me. Amanda rushes stage left, stage
right, fretting over misplaced props,
broken lights.

Mr. Turner asks Mrs. Littlebaum,
a Special Ed teacher, to help me perfect
my signing. Mrs. Littlebaum adjusts
her bifocals, wags a finger at my *W*,
and every other letter I attempt.

I'm starting to understand how frustrated
Annie felt in the Keller house.
This show is not exactly the party
with my friends I imagined.

It will be a minor miracle if I manage
an hour's sleep tonight between rehearsal
till ten and six hours of procrastinated
papers lining my backpack.
And today is only Wednesday.

Thursday

Amanda and Gina lean against my locker,
each with a pink gerbera daisy in hand.
"You're doing such a great job in the play."
Amanda kisses my cheek. Gina passes me
her flower. A smile slides across her face.
"That Mrs. Littlebaum must be destroyed."
Amanda's left arm hooks around my shoulder
and my eyes turn into sprinklers, a stream
of water down each cheek. Students pass
like subway cars, left and right. A few slow,
ponder my tears, but I don't care,
tears of happiness complement my outfit,
suit me just fine.

Something I Need to Remember: Sunbathing (Back When We Were Best Friends)

The summer we were fourteen
I had nothing better to do than help
Gina and her two younger, scraggly brothers
repaint their house. I thought it was fantastic
because no one told us what to do,
they just handed me a brush. At my house,
Mom would have printed instructions,
modeled how to dip the brush in paint,
and watched my every stroke.

Painting was hard work and after an hour
Gina's brothers grew restless, dumped
a can of paint in the yard, and started
howling when the dog licked the grass
and got a green tongue. Gina's dad stormed
outside, chased her brothers with fist in air.
"To hell with this." Gina whisked me
into her bedroom. She tossed me a blue
floral bikini, my first ever, and said,
"The sun's best from eleven to one, anyway."

I was falling top and bottom
out of her two-piece, but Gina said
I looked "older" and hoisted me up
onto the roof's black shingles. "Don't sit down,"
she warned. "You'll get burned."
She threw me a towel, a bottle of water,
and slathered baby oil on her legs.

Her neighborhood was quieter twenty feet
off the ground. You could no longer see
her father's piecemeal Chevette corroding
the driveway or the junk in Gina's lawn.
"It's cool up here," I said and closed my eyes.
Gina fanned out on her reflective mat.
"This is my favorite place. I'm glad you're here."

Before-Break Tan

Friday before spring break
Gina stands at her locker,
struggles to find room
to accommodate her History tome.

I tap her shoulder. "You're
leaving for Florida on Monday,
right?" She nods and I hand her
an envelope full of certificates

to her favorite tanning salon,
Tantastic. "I made us a ten
o'clock appointment tomorrow,
if you're not busy," I say.

Gina just stares at me.
"I've been thinking about
freshman summer, how you
taught me to cultivate the perfect tan."

Gina's still silent and I'm
beginning to feel like my mother,
the monologue queen. "I miss you,
Gina. I think our friendship

got lost somewhere.
And because we never really
talked about it, things sometimes
get weird between us."

Gina nods and says, "I know."
I point to the envelope.
"So do you want to work on a base
tomorrow or what?"

Gina smiles. "Yeah."

Early Morning

the first words
my throat forms crackle.
They're rusty, hard to spit out.
But after ten minutes
and a glass of water,
I find my voice
normalizes.
It's strong, agile
and all mine—
sounds like no one else.

Easter Baskets, Bonnets, and Eggs

Mom's a traditionalist,
all holidays equipped

with their specific attire,
decor, and food. She enlists
Dad's services on the ladder

to hang wooden pastel eggs
on the front-lawn tree,
changes the table linens
to Martha Stewart lemon

and asks that I pick out gloves
and hat to wear to Easter services
from her carefully stowed assortment.
On Good Friday, Grandma
comes over and we decorate eggs.

Mom lines every imaginable
contraption to color and style
Easter eggs on the kitchen table,
from vinegar and food coloring
to elaborate stencil sets. Dad
mathematically stripes his egg

in five equal bands. Grandma
hand-paints a rose on her egg.
I change my mind about my base
color so many times I end up
with a purplish monster that I draw
a face on and name Doris. Mom
creates simple solid-colored eggs

in pink, lemon, and baby blue,
arranges them in the centerpiece
basket. She confesses that she
cheated and "predyed" some eggs
this morning. Mom sets a small
wicker basket on the table
that holds three eggs, each
with a single perfectly calligraphed

word: *The, Miracle,* and *Worker.*
A couple months ago, this sort
of gesture would make me gag,
roll my eyes, and want to toss
her motherly intentions down
the disposal. Her eggs are a touch
corny, but I say, "Mom, those are really
cool, thanks," and I can see in her eyes
that I said the exact right words.

MAY ⌇

is possibility, permission,
a wish that tips my tongue

like the echo
of a baby's first word.

The first time I heard
my voice over a tape recorder

it sounded strange, high,
lilac at the edge of a soft squeal.

It was foreign to me, certainly
not the voice I heard in my head

and I wondered,
"Is that how I really sound?"

But after years of camcorders
and microphones I now recognize

my voice in playback,
claim it as my own.

Yellow Roses

Walking home from Derek's
I pass a white house lined with roses,
a parade of bushes skirting the backyard,
and I think about Robin, how she hated
yellow roses, told me never to send anyone
yellow roses, because they meant death.

A week before Robin checked into the hospital
I spent the night at her house. A vase of six
yellow roses adorned her nightstand.
I asked Robin who sent them, but she changed
the subject to Gina and I forgot
about the flowers. Three days later
when I picked her up for school,
her room smelled stale and coppery.
I noticed the roses sagging in brown water.
I told her she ought to get rid of them.
Robin turned away and said, "Yeah, I know."

Withered roses beside her bed,
the retreat of Robin's voice—
How did I miss the clues, fail to see
the hurricane tearing Robin down?

Staring at this yellow rosebush,
Robin's words beat in my ears,
"Yellow roses mean death."
My pace quickens, the scent of rose petals,
their sweetness on the breeze
makes me want to vomit,
and for the first time in weeks
I can't get the sound of Robin's voice
out of my head.

Family Recipe

"Mom, let's bake double-fudge brownies,"
I pull down the mixing bowl, measuring
cups, load the counter with ingredients.
"I'm feeling chocolate deprived."

Mom doesn't believe in electric mixers,
combines everything slowly by hand.
Rich cocoa wafts through the house,
the kitchen heat a blanket on my shoulders.

Brownies in oven, I try to concentrate
on chemistry homework. Mom asks if I want
to practice lines. I shut my book, hand her
a script, nestle beside her on the sofa, and say,

"It's amazing Helen didn't just give up on life."
Mom smiles. "You're thinking about Robin,
huh?" I nod. Mom's sharp. The timer buzzes.
Brownies emerge oozing chocolate chips.

Even though technically they are too hot
to cut, Mom slices into the pan.
One decadent mouthful and I am transported.
I wish I could mail this feeling to Robin.

What I Might Say if Robin Were Here

There is a type of friend I want to be,
not the doll of limited speech
who talks only when you pull her string.

Not some plastic shell whose eyes
roll back in her head and remain
closed half the time.

I'm looking for words, Robin, words
to share when our days are charcoal
and vermilion, fuchsia, and bronze.

Act III: Homecoming

In the final act
Annie says she needs
a teacher
needs an answer key
that diagrams
how to unlock language
for Helen,
open Helen's mind.

Annie needs compassion,
she thinks
she needs more time.
But the hourglass
sand's depleted, no more solitary
instruction time remains.

Helen reinserts herself
into the world.
The Keller gates swing open,
welcome
the lost child home.

The Message

When I arrive home from rehearsal
Mom says there is a message on the machine
from Robin. I want to do a one-eighty
and drive to another house, but I plop down
into desk chair. Mom asks if I want to talk.
I shake my head, "Maybe later."

Robin was released last week,
but I didn't think she'd call me. Yet.
Didn't think I was ready to hear
her actual voice.
Things were going so well
with Derek, the play, school.
I almost wished Robin would never return.

Robin's voice booms out the speaker,
sounds odd. "Hi, Sarah, it's Robin.
Want to let you know I'm back and I'm okay.
I'd really like to talk to you."
Long scary pause.
"Could you meet me tomorrow after school
at Mel's? Leave me a message
and let me know."

A Date with Disaster?

I pace bedroom floor, punch the digits
to Robin's home phone,
if she answers what will I say?
After three rings I'm ready to hang up,
pretend I never got her message,
when Robin's recorded voice clicks on,
"I'm not here or not answering.
You know what to do."

A few seconds after the beep,
I mutter, "Okay, I'll meet you
tomorrow at Mel's."

I clunk down phone receiver,
what did I just agree to do?
I'm quivering, shaking scared
to talk to Robin. I feel light-headed,
seeing Robin might be like
hand-delivering my soul to the devil,
a disastrously bad decision.

My fingers hover over phone keys,
ready to bail out.

I wonder what Robin looks like
post-therapy, how she's doing, if
in any alternate universe we might be
friends again. I wonder if she missed me
as much as her nail polish, or as much as
I missed her.

I walk away from the phone.
If I close my eyes I glimpse
this fuzzy picture of senior year,
Robin and me driving to school.
In my daydream I don't hold back
my sentences. In my daydream
Robin's smiling.

A Little Help from My Friends

When I announce at lunch
that I'm meeting Robin
after school, and I predict
that when I push through Mel's
front door, I may create
a new kind of natural disaster,

Gina offers to lend me
her rain poncho, Derek digs
through his backpack
to find me a flashlight,
and Amanda promises to pray
repeatedly for my safe return.

They all nod in agreement,
it's a good thing for me
to talk to Robin. The lunch trio
assures me that I can handle
whatever weather, good or inclement,
I might encounter after school.

First Contact

I hesitate, my hand freezes on metal
push-bar of Mel's front door.
Through the plate glass I see
Robin seated in our old booth.

As I inch into restaurant, weave
through Mel's mostly empty tables,
I notice that Robin's not smoking,
and she wears a deep blue crewneck,
not her customary black.

Robin squints up at me, waves
as I approach the table. Her wrist
crisscrossed with Band-Aids,
she tucks her hand quickly under thigh.

"Hi," I say and wriggle into booth.
"Have you been waiting long?"

"Yeah," she says. "But I got here early."

I fiddle with coffee spoon.
Like she's some sort of solar eclipse,
I can't look directly at Robin.

"Well, they tell me I'm better,"
Robin says and lights up a smoke.

I stir half-and-half into my coffee.
"That's good."

"Better," she mutters on an exhale.
"How do I look to you?"

My eyes scan Robin, her roots
need dye, her skin's tinged violet.
She looks worn down, used up,
smaller somehow, like the stub
of my favorite eyeliner pencil.
"I don't know," I say.
"I haven't seen you in a long time."

"Yeah," she says, a familiar,
bitter tinge haunting her voice.

We sit silent as stagnant water,
not even our breathing audible.

I stare at her bandaged wrist,
cradling coffee cup.

I drop a five on the table,
explain that I'm due at rehearsal,
she and I will have to catch up later.

Twilight Just Before Rehearsal

Tulips bloom in the courtyard
behind the theater. Gina and Amanda
kick off shoes, sprawl in fading sunlight
before they're forced to enter
the cave of the auditorium.
When I join them, Gina asks,
"How did it go with Robin?"

"It went," I say and the tears
erupt down my face. "She's
different. I'm different."

Amanda hands me a tissue.
"Just let it out. You'll feel better."

"But see, this is exactly what's
so frustrating. I'm crying over Robin
with you. Why couldn't I cry with her?"
I crumple the tissue in my fist;
I know the answer.
"Because she's not really my friend.
I don't know if she ever was."

Amanda shakes her head, tells me
that my friendship with Robin
post-hospital just requires
special handling, a pair of satin gloves,
compassion, and good old-fashioned time.

I smooth my jeans. "No, Amanda,
I don't think so. We were destructive,
Robin and me, from the beginning.
Some friendships are meant to be retired."

A stagehand screams to Amanda
from the auditorium's open side door,
Mr. Turner needs her ASAP.
Amanda nods, hugs me, zips into theater.

Gina slides sunglasses atop her head.
No doubt she votes in favor
of extinguishing the Robin friendship.

Gina brushes herself off,
slings her coat over shoulder,
"I don't know what exactly went down
with you and Robin, but you and I fixed
a fairly damaged friendship."

"It's not the same," I say.
"I'm not sure I want to be Robin's friend."

"Sarah, if it's worth it to you,
you'll figure out how to be friends
with Robin." Gina grabs my hand,
pulls me to my feet. "If not, fine."

Dress Rehearsal

The lights come up, my hands work hard,
nimble servants spelling language into Helen's
palms, words I tender for her touch and grasp.

Scurrying around stage in a long gray dress,
dark glasses, and scratchy wool shawl,
I miss my twenty-first-century attire—
cotton shirts, jeans, no corsets lacing my waist.

In this costume, with her words in my mouth,
I feel close to Annie Sullivan. But I bring
my body's limitations with me on stage,
the particular way my eyes peer over glasses,
my stiff shoulders confronting the supper table.

I have resisted renting *The Miracle Worker*
on DVD, don't want to mimic Anne Bancroft's
award-winning accent and posture, the words
she emphasizes, the words she lets fall away.
I've done a copycat routine before. This time
I choose to find Annie myself, find myself in Annie.

The Sarah Lewis on Derek Crawford's Couch

I drape my arm around Derek,
can't focus on anything but the curve
of his neck into shoulder, his hand
grazing my thigh.

The last six weeks seem to have zoomed by,
days like meteors crashing the earth's
atmosphere—sometimes terrifying, damaging,
but mostly brilliant, a star shower lighting the sky.

There are mornings I check my driver's license.
How could the Sarah Lewis of a thousand
black turtlenecks land the guy cradled
next to me on the couch, and the lead in the play,
a winsome smile exploding across my face?
Statistically, change causes stress, but today
I feel good enough to bathing-suit shop.

I stopped hiding behind long sweater sleeves,
exposed myself to a few ultraviolet rays
and let people see a little of the Sarah
behind makeup and wardrobe.
Not everyone loves what I can show them.
But a few oddballs, myself included,
are beginning to really like Sarah Lewis.

Invitation

Dear Robin,

I dialed your number five times, kept hanging up. I hope you can hear my words on this page, because what I didn't say to you at Mel's is everything.

It felt like someone chopped off my right hand when I heard you tried to kill yourself. My body fell numb, you were severed from me, but your ghost limb haunted my every move. Each breath I drew tasted like guilt. I needed to talk to you, but you cut my phone cord. Still I missed you, worried about you, wondered why you did it.

You played dead with me. I had no option but to mourn and move on. Where I moved to, Robin, is this really cool place, this unexpected place I didn't know I could find, where I like the sound of my voice, tolerate my reflection in the mirror. I had to travel to this place by myself, but I don't live here alone.

The species of friends we were before is extinct to me. Skeletons of disappointment and unhappiness don't fit me anymore. I doubt those old bones feel comfortable to you either.

What I'm saying is that maybe we can start over, forge new footprints. I'd love it if you came to see me in the play tomorrow night, but understand if you don't want to or can't. I can't go back, Robin, only forward now. I'm inviting you to come along.

Sarah